Kate Hoffmann's Mighty Quinns are back—and this time, they're going D

All Quinn males, ... legend of the firs... all been warned a... only thing ca... ...ng down a Quinn is a woman.

These sexy Aussie brothers are about to learn that they can't escape their family legacy, no matter where they live. And they're about to enjoy every satisfying minute of it!

Watch for:

THE MIGHTY QUINNS: BRODY
June 2009

THE MIGHTY QUINNS: TEAGUE
July 2009

THE MIGHTY QUINNS: CALLUM
August 2009

Blaze

Dear Reader,

I'm falling in love with Australian men! And yet I've never met one in person. There are certainly a number of dishy dudes from Down Under to watch on television and in the movies, but I've got a crush on the Quinns. Maybe that's why I can't seem to stop writing about them.

Setting a trilogy in Australia posed a unique set of problems. Though Australians speak the same language that we do here in the States, they put their own unique and colorful spin on English. I've had some wonderful help from Aussie author Sarah Mayberry in working out the lingo and a lot of the day-to-day details of life. And I'll leave it to my wonderful Australian readers to let me know if I've gotten it right.

I hope you enjoy the second installment of THE MIGHTY QUINNS saga. Callum is up next month, and then I'm heading off on a tour of the world to see if I can find any more interesting Quinns to write about.

Happy reading,

Kate

Kate Hoffmann

THE MIGHTY QUINNS: TEAGUE

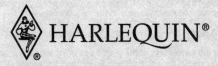

HARLEQUIN®

TORONTO • NEW YORK • LONDON
AMSTERDAM • PARIS • SYDNEY • HAMBURG
STOCKHOLM • ATHENS • TOKYO • MILAN • MADRID
PRAGUE • WARSAW • BUDAPEST • AUCKLAND

Recycling programs
for this product may
not exist in your area.

ISBN-13: 978-0-373-79486-7

THE MIGHTY QUINNS: TEAGUE

ABOUT THE AUTHOR

Kate Hoffmann has been writing for Harlequin Books for fifteen years and has published nearly sixty books, including Harlequin Temptation novels, Harlequin Blaze books, novellas and even the occasional historical. When she isn't writing, she is involved in various musical and theatrical activities in her small Wisconsin community. She enjoys sleeping late, drinking coffee and eating bonbons. She lives with her two cats, Tally and Chloe, and her computer, which shall remain nameless.

Books by Kate Hoffmann

To Dr. Greg B., DVM, for his insights
on equine veterinary medicine.
And for taking such good care of
Chloe and Tally!

Prologue

TEAGUE QUINN STRETCHED his arms over his head and closed his eyes against the sun, the warm rays heating the big rock beneath him. The wind rustled in the dry brush. The sounds of the outback were so familiar they were almost like music to him.

He'd managed to escape the house before anyone noticed he was gone, saddling his horse and riding out in a cloud of dust, the shoe box tucked under his arm. When he wasn't working the stock with his father and brothers, he was tending to some other job his mother had conjured out of thin air. He wondered what it might be like to live a normal life, in a grand house in Brisbane, where daily chores didn't exist.

There'd be girls and parties and school and sports— all the things fourteen-year-old boys were supposed to enjoy. Teague sighed. Most boys his age didn't like school, but real classrooms with real teachers, chemistry and biology and physics and math, these were things he'd never experienced.

Instead, Teague was stuck on a cattle station in Queensland, with his parents, his two brothers and a rowdy bunch of jackaroos. Classes took place at the kitchen table, him and his brothers gathered around the radio listening to School of the Air. The closest town, Bilbarra, had a library and a small school, but that was a two-hour drive, much too far to make it practical day to day. Some of the kids on the more profitable stations were sent away to boarding school, but Kerry Creek wasn't exactly swimming in cash. Though the Quinn family wasn't poor, they weren't in the big bickies, either.

Teague heard the sound of hoofbeats and pushed up on his elbows, scanning the approach to the big rock and cursing to himself. Would he ever be able to get away from his brothers, or would they be following him around the rest of his life?

When he didn't see a rider coming from the direction of the homestead, he glanced over his shoulder and watched as a horse galloped full bore from the opposite direction, its rider hunched low in the saddle. Scrambling to his feet, Teague stood on the rock, ready to defend his territory against the interloper.

The boy drew his horse to a stop, the animal breathing heavily. From beneath the brim of a battered stockman's hat, he stared at Teague, a grim expression on his face. He wasn't very big, Teague mused, sizing up his chances if it came down to a fistfight.

But then suddenly, the boy smiled. "Did I scare you?" In one smooth motion, he brushed his hat from his head and a tumble of wavy blond hair revealed not a boy, but a girl. His breath caught in his throat as he stared into her pale blue eyes. Teague swallowed hard. She was the most beautiful girl he'd ever seen.

"I scared the piss out of you, didn't I? You should see your face. You're as pale as a ghost."

Teague scowled, embarrassed that she'd noticed his reaction. "Nick off. I wasn't scared. Why would I be scared of a mite like you? You couldn't knock the skin off a rice pudding."

She slid off her horse. "Oh, yeah. Well, you're so stupid, you couldn't tell your arse from a hole in the ground."

Teague opened his mouth, shocked to hear that kind of language from a girl. But then, he really had no experience talking to girls. With no sisters, he wasn't sure how girls were supposed to talk. On the telly, they always seemed to act so proper and prissy. This girl was acting more like his brothers.

She hitched her hands on her waist and stared up at him. "Well, are you going to give me a hand up or are you going to be mingy about the view?"

Teague studied her for a long moment. There wasn't much to fear from her. She was at least a head shorter than him and a few stone lighter. Though, in a verbal sparring match, she'd probably slice him into dinner for the dingoes. He reluctantly held out his hand and pulled her up beside him.

She scrambled to her feet and took a good look around. A frown wrinkled her brow, then she plopped down and sighed deeply.

"You don't like the view?"

She shook her head. "I thought I might be able to see the ocean."

Teague laughed, but when he saw the hurt in her eyes, he realized the depth of her disappointment. "Sorry," he mumbled as he sat down beside her. "You can't see the ocean from anywhere on this station. Even if you get up to the highest point. It's too far away."

She cursed beneath her breath before turning away from him. "I used to live near the ocean. I could see the water every day. I wish I could see it again."

A long silence grew between them. "That must have been nice," he finally ventured.

"It was better than living out here. Everything is so…dusty. And there are flies everywhere."

"Yeah, but you don't get to ride horses in the city," Teague offered, surprised to find himself defending the outback. "Or keep cattle. Or have a lot of dogs. And you don't see lizards and 'roos like you do here."

"You like animals?" she asked, her disappointment forgotten as suddenly as it had appeared.

Teague nodded. "Last month I found a bird with a broken wing. And I healed it." He pointed to the box beside him. "I'm going to let it go today."

"Can I see?" she asked, bending over the box.

Teague picked the box up, said a silent prayer, then lifted the lid. The sparrow immediately took flight and the girl clapped her hands as it flew into the distance. He felt his cheeks warm. "Maybe it healed itself. It's only a sparrow, but I kept it alive until it could fly again. I find hurt animals all the time and I know how to make them well again." He paused. "I like doing that."

A tiny smile tugged at her lips. "All right, there is one good thing about living on Wallaroo."

Teague swallowed hard, wondering if she'd just paid him a compliment. Then her words sank in. "You live on Wallaroo?" He hadn't even considered the possibility. But now that he thought about it, this was the girl his parents had had been talking about. "You're Hayley Fraser, then."

She seemed surprised he knew her name. "Maybe," she replied.

He'd heard the story by way of eavesdropping. Hayley's parents had been killed in an auto wreck when she was eight years old. She'd been moved from foster home to foster home, until her grandfather had finally agreed to take her. According to Teague's mum, old man Fraser hadn't been on speaking terms with his only child since Jake Fraser had run away from home at age eighteen. And now, his poor granddaughter was forced to live with a cold, unfeeling man who'd never wanted her on Wallaroo in the first place.

Teague's mum had insisted that Wallaroo was no place for a troubled young girl to grow up, without any women on the station at all, and with only rowdy men to serve as an example. Yet there was nothing anyone could do for her. Except him, Teague mused.

"You ride pretty good," he said. "Who taught you?"

"I taught myself. It doesn't take much skill. You hop on the horse and hang on."

"You know your granddad and my father are ene-mies. They hate each other."

Hayley blinked as she glanced over at him. "No surprise. Harry hates everyone, including me."

"You call him Harry?"

She shrugged. "That's his name."

Teague felt an odd lurch in his stomach as his eyes met hers. She had the longest eyelashes he'd ever seen. His gaze drifted down to her mouth and suddenly, he found himself wondering what it might be like to kiss such a bold and brave girl.

"It's because of that land right over there," Teague said, pointing toward the horizon. "It belongs to Kerry Creek, but Har—your grandfather thinks it belongs to him. Every few years old man Fraser goes to court and tries to take it back, but he always loses."

"Why does he keep trying?"

"He says that my great-grandfather gave it to his father. It's part of the Quinn homestead, so I don't know why any Quinn would ever give it away. I think your grandfather might be a bit batty."

Hayley turned and looked in the direction that he was pointing, apparently unfazed by his opinion of her grandfather. "Who'd care about that land? There's nothing on it."

"Water," he said, leaning closer and drawing a deep breath. She even smelled good, he mused. He reached up and touched her hair, curious to see if it was as soft as it looked, but Hayley jumped, turning to him with a suspicious expression.

"What are you doing?"

"Nothing!" Teague said. "You had a bug in your hair. I picked it out."

She sighed softly. "I better get home. He'll wonder where I am. I have to get supper ready."

Teague slid off the rock, dropping lightly to his feet. Then he held his hands up and Hayley nimbly jumped down. His hands rested on her waist as Teague took in the details of her face, trying to memorize them all before she disappeared.

Hayley quickly stepped away from him, as if shocked by his touch. "Maybe I'll see you again," she murmured, looking uneasy.

"Maybe. I'm here a lot. I guess if you came out tomorrow night after supper, you might see me."

"Maybe I would." She glanced up at him through thick lashes and smiled hesitantly. Then she gave him a little wave and ran to her horse. Teague held his breath as she hitched her foot in the stirrup and swung her leg over the saddle. "So what's your name?" she asked as she wove the reins through her fingers.

"Teague," he said. "Teague Quinn."

She set her hat on her head, pushing it down low over her eyes. "Nice to meet you, Teague Quinn." With that, Hayley wheeled the horse around and a moment later, she was riding back in the direction from which she'd come.

"Shit," he muttered. Now he knew exactly what his mother had been talking about when she'd insisted that someday he'd meet a girl who would knock him off his feet.

"Hayley Fraser." He liked saying her name. It sounded new and exciting. Someday, he was going to marry that girl.

1

THE DUST FROM the dirt road billowed out behind Teague's Range Rover. He glanced at the speedometer, then decided the suspension could take a bit more abuse. Adding pressure to the accelerator, he fixed his gaze down the rutted road.

He'd finished his rounds and had just landed on the Kerry Creek airstrip when the phone call had come in. Doc Daley was in the midst of a tricky C-section on Lanie Pittman's bulldog at the Bilbarra surgery, and needed him to cover the call. It was only after Teague asked for details that he realized his services might not be welcomed. The request had come from Wallaroo Station.

The Frasers and the Quinns had been at it for as long as he could remember, their feud igniting over a piece of disputed land—land that contained the best water bore on either station.

In the outback, water was as good as gold and it was worth fighting for. Cattle and horses couldn't survive without it, and without cattle or horses the family station wasn't worth a zack. Teague wasn't sure how or why the land was in dispute after all these years, only that the fight never seemed to end. His grandfather had fought the Frasers, as had his father, and now, his older brother, Callum.

But all that would have to be forgotten now that he was venturing into enemy territory. He had come to help an animal in distress. And if old man Fraser refused his help, well, he'd give it anyway.

As Teague navigated the rough road, his thoughts spun back nearly ten years, to the last time he'd visited Wallaroo. He felt a stab of regret at the memory, a vivid image of Hayley Fraser burned into his brain.

It had been the most difficult day of his life. He'd been heading off into a brand-new world—university in Perth, hundreds of miles from the girl he loved. She'd promised to join him the moment she turned eighteen. They'd both get part-time jobs and they'd attend school together. He hadn't known that it was the last time he'd ever see her.

For weeks afterward, his letters had gone unanswered. Every time he rang her, he ended up in an argument with her grandfather, who refused to call her to the phone. And when he finally returned during his term break, Hayley was gone.

Even now, his memories of her always spun back to the girl she'd been at seventeen and not the woman she'd become. That woman on the telly wasn't really Hayley, at least not the Hayley he knew.

The runaway teenager with the honey-blond hair and the pale blue eyes had ended up in Sydney. According to the press, she'd been "discovered" working at a

T-shirt shop near Bondi Beach. A month later, she'd debuted as a scheming teenage vixen on one of Australia's newest nighttime soap operas. And seven years later, she was the star of one of the most popular programs on Aussie television.

He'd thought about calling her plenty of times when he'd visited Sydney. He'd been curious, wondering if there would be any attraction left between them. Probably not, considering she'd dated some of Australia's most famous bachelors—two or three footballers, a pro tennis player, a couple of rock stars and more actors than he cared to count. No, she probably hadn't thought of Teague in years.

As he approached the homestead, Teague was stunned at the condition of the house. Harry Fraser used to take great pride in the station, but it was clear that his attitude had changed. Teague watched as a stooped figure rose from a chair on the ramshackle porch, dressed in a stained work shirt and dirty jeans. The old man's thick white hair stood on end. Teague's breath caught as he noticed the rifle in Harry's hand.

"Shit," he muttered, pulling the Range Rover to a stop. Drawing a deep breath, he opened the window. His reflexes were good and the SUV was fast, but Harry Fraser had been a crack shot in his day. "Put the gun down, Mr. Fraser."

Harry squinted. "Who is that? State your name or get off my property."

"I'm the vet you sent for," Teague said, slowly realizing that Harry couldn't make him out. His eyesight was clearly failing and they hadn't spoken in so many years there was no way Harry would recognize his voice. "Doc Daley sent me. He's in the middle of a surgery and couldn't get away. I'm…new."

Harry lowered the rifle, then shuffled back to his chair. "She's in the stable," he said, pointing feebly in the direction of one of the crumbling sheds. "It's colic. There isn't much to do, I reckon." He waved the gun at him. "I'm not payin' you if the horse dies. Got that?"

They'd discuss the fee later, after Harry had been disarmed and Teague had a chance to examine the patient. He steered the Range Rover toward the smallest of the old sheds, remembering that it used to serve as the stables on Wallaroo. Besides that old shack on the border between Wallaroo and Kerry Creek, the stables had been one of their favorite meeting places, a spot where he and Hayley had spent many clandestine hours exploring the wonders of each other's bodies.

Teague pulled the truck to a stop at the wide shed door, then grabbed his bag and hopped out. The shed was in worse condition than the house. "Hullo!" he shouted, wondering if there were any station hands about.

To his surprise, a female voice replied. "Back here. Last stall."

He strode through the empty stable, each stall filled with moldering straw. A rat scurried in front of him and he stopped and watched as it wriggled through a hole in the wall. While the rodent startled him, it was nothing compared to the shock he felt when he stepped inside the stall.

Hayley Fraser knelt beside a horse lying on a fresh bed of straw. She was dressed in a flannel shirt and jeans, the toes of her boots peaking out beneath the ragged hems of her pant legs. They stared at each other for a long time, neither one of them able to speak. It wasn't supposed to be like this, Teague thought, his mind racing. He'd always imagined they'd meet on a busy street or in a restaurant.

Suddenly, as if a switch had been flipped, she blinked and pointed to the horse. "It's Molly," she said, her voice wavering. "I'm pretty sure she has colic. I don't know what else to do. I can't get her up."

Teague stepped past Hayley and bent down next to the animal. The mare was covered with sweat and her nostrils were flared. He stepped aside as the horse rolled, a sign that Hayley's diagnosis was probably right. Teague stood and reached into the feed bin, grabbing a handful of grain and sniffing it. "Moldy," he said, turning to Hayley.

"I got here last night," she explained, peering into the grain bin. "When I came in this morning she was like this."

"She might have an impaction. How long has she been down?"

"I don't know," Hayley said. "I found her like this at ten this morning."

Teague drew a deep breath. Colic in horses was tricky to treat. It could either be cured in a matter of hours or it could kill the horse. "We need to get her up. I'll give her some pain medication, then we'll dose her with mineral oil and see if that helps."

"What if it doesn't?" Hayley asked. "What about surgery?"

Teague shook his head. "I can't do surgery here. And the nearest equine surgical facility is at the university in Brisbane."

"I don't care what it costs," she said, a desperate edge to her voice. "I don't care if I need to charter a jet to fly her there. I'll do whatever it takes."

He chuckled softly at the notion of putting the horse on a jet. "We'll cross that fence when we come to it," Teague murmured. "Help me get her up."

It took them a full ten minutes of tugging and prodding and slapping and shouting before Molly struggled to her feet, her eyes wild and her flanks trembling. The moment she got up, she made another move to go down and Teague shouted to distract her, slapping her on the chest and pushing her out of the stall.

He handed the lead to Hayley. "Keep her walking, don't let her go down again. I've got to fetch some supplies."

Teague ran toward the stable door, then glanced over his shoulder to see Hayley struggling with the mare. Thank God they had this to focus on, he mused. It was difficult enough seeing her again without demanding answers to his questions and explanations for her behavior.

He opened up the tailgate on the Range Rover and searched through the plastic bins until he found a bag of IV fluid, which he shoved in his jacket pocket. He took a vial of Banamine from the case of medication. Then he grabbed the rest of the supplies he needed—a hypodermic, IV tubing, a nasogastric tube and a jug of mineral oil—and put everything into a wooden crate.

When he got back to the stable, he saw Hayley kneeling on the dirty concrete floor with Molly lying beside her.

She looked up, tears streaming down her cheeks. "I couldn't stop her. She just went down."

Teague set the crate on a nearby bale of straw, then gently helped Hayley to her feet. In all the years he'd known her, he'd never seen Hayley cry. Not a single tear, not even when she'd fallen from her horse or scraped her knee. He'd never thought much about it until now, but it must have taken a great deal of strength to control her emotions for so long.

"Don't worry," he said, giving her hands a reassuring squeeze. "We'll get her up."

Then he brushed the pale hair from her eyes, his thumbs damp from her tears. It had been so long since he'd touched her, so many years since he'd looked into those eyes. But it seemed like only yesterday. All the old feelings were bubbling up inside him. His instinct to protect her had kicked in the moment he looked into her eyes and he found himself more worried about Hayley than the horse.

Teague didn't bother to think about the consequences before kissing her. It was the right thing to do, a way to soothe her fears and stop her tears. He bent closer and touched his lips to hers, gently exploring with his tongue until she opened beneath the assault.

Cupping her face in his hands, he molded her mouth to his, stunned by the flood of desire racing through him. They were teenagers again, the two of them caught up in a heady mix of hormones they couldn't control and emotions they didn't understand.

He drew back and smiled. "Better?" Hayley nodded mutely and Teague looked down at the horse. "Then let's get to work."

It was as if the kiss had focused their thoughts and strengthened their bond. Though he wanted to kiss her again, he had professional duties to dispatch first. And saving Molly was more important than indulging in desire. They managed to get the horse on her feet again and pushed her up against a wall to keep her still as Teague inserted the IV catheter into her neck. Drawing out a measure of the painkiller, he injected it into the IV bag.

"There. She should start feeling a little better. Once she does, we'll dose her with mineral oil. If it's an impaction, that should help."

They walked back and forth, the length of the stable, both of them holding on to Molly's halter. At each turn, he took the time to glance over at her, letting his gaze linger.

Without all the slinky clothes and the fancy makeup and hair, she didn't look anything like a television star. She looked exactly like the fresh-faced girl he used to kiss and touch, the first girl he'd ever had sex with and the last girl he'd ever loved. Teague clenched his free hand into a fist, fighting the urge to pull her into his arms and kiss her again.

"So you got home yesterday," he said.

Hayley nodded, continuing to stare straight ahead. He could read the wariness in her expression. If she was feeling half of what he was, then her heart was probably pounding and her mind spinning with the aftereffects of the kiss they'd shared.

"I've seen you on telly. You've become quite a good actress." This brought a smile, a step in the right direction, Teague thought. "I heard you won some award?"

"A Logie award. And I didn't win. I've been nominated three times. Haven't won yet."

"That's good, though, right? Nominated is good. Better than not being nominated."

"It's a soap opera," she said. "It's not like I'm doing Shakespeare with the Royal Queensland."

"But you could, if you wanted to, right?"

Hayley shook her head. "No, I don't have any formal training. They hired me on *Castle Cove* because I looked like the part. Not because I could act."

He wanted to ask why she had decided to run away from home. And why she hadn't come to him as they'd always planned. Teague drew a deep breath, then stopped. Molly had settled down, her respiration now almost normal. "See, she's feeling better," he said, smoothing his palm over the horse's muzzle. "That's the thing with colic. One minute the horse is close to death and the next she's on the mend. Have you ever twitched a horse?"

Hayley shook her head. "I don't want you to do that. It will hurt her."

"It looks painful, but it isn't if it's done properly. It's going to release endorphins and it will relax Molly so she won't fight the tube."

"All right," she said, nodding. "I trust you."

Three simple words. *I trust you.* But they meant the

world to him. After all that had happened between them, and all that hadn't, maybe things weren't so bad after all.

As they tended to Molly, they barely spoke, Teague calmly giving her instructions when needed. Hayley murmured softly to keep her calm, smoothing her hand along Molly's neck. Once the mineral oil was pumped into the horse's stomach, Teague removed the tube and the twitch and they began to walk her again.

"She is feeling better," Hayley said. "I can see it already." She looked over at him. "Thank you."

Teague saw the tears swimming in her eyes again and he fought the urge to gather her into his arms and hold her. The mere thought of touching her was enough to send a flood of heat pulsing through his veins.

He'd kiss Hayley again, only this time it wouldn't be to soothe her fears, but to make her remember how good it had been between them. And how good it could be again.

HAYLEY STARED OUT at the setting sun, her back resting against the side of the stable. A bale of straw served as a low bench. Teague sat beside her with his long legs crossed in front of him and his stockman's hat pulled low to protect his eyes from the glare.

They'd spent the last hour walking Molly around the stable yard, and to Hayley's great relief, the mare seemed to be recovering quite well. Hayley wanted to throw herself into Teague's arms and kiss him silly with gratitude. But she knew doing that would only unleash feelings that had been buried for a very long time—feelings that could sweep them both into dangerous waters.

She'd already turned into an emotional wreck over Molly. Since she'd returned to Wallaroo, she'd rediscovered her emotional side. It had disappeared after her parents died, when she'd stubbornly refused to surrender to sorrow or pain. But in these familiar surroundings, her past had slowly come back and she'd found herself grieving, for her parents' deaths, for her difficult adolescence and for her fractured relationship with Harry.

There was no telling what might happen if she and Teague revisited their past. With so many unresolved feelings, so many mistakes she'd made, she'd likely cry for days.

Now, it seemed so clear, his leaving. He'd been going off to university, starting his life away from home. But at the time she'd seen it as a betrayal, a desertion. Though she'd known he'd be back, Hayley's insecurities had overwhelmed her without Teague to help hold them in check.

From the moment she'd met Teague, she'd found a home, a family and someone she could trust. She'd come to depend on him. He had been the only person who loved her, the only person who cared that she existed and suddenly he was gone. She'd been angry. And though she'd tried to tell herself she'd be all right on her own, she'd been terrified.

So she'd run, away from the place that held so many memories, away from the boy who might not want to return.

She snuck a glance at him. He'd grown into a handsome man. Working in television, she'd met a lot of good-looking blokes, but none of them possessed Teague's raw masculinity. Teague Quinn was a flesh-and-blood man, seemingly unaware of the powerful effect he had on women.

"She looks almost frisky," Teague commented, nodding toward the horse.

"I don't know how I'll ever be able to thank you," Hayley said.

"Don't worry. I'm glad I could help. I know how much Molly means to you. I remember the day you got her."

"My sixteenth birthday," Hayley said. "My grandfather was never one for birthday celebrations. He'd shove money into my hand and tell me not to spend it on silly things. And then, he gave me Molly and I thought everything had changed."

"You rode her over to Kerry Creek to show me. You looked so happy, I thought you'd burst. You immediately challenged me to a race."

"Which I won, as I remember."

"Which I let you win, since it was your birthday. You were such a wild child. Looking back, I wonder how you managed to survive to adulthood. Remember when you were determined to jump the gate near the shack? You were sure Molly could do it. You even bet me my new saddle against your Christmas money."

"That wasn't my finest hour," Hayley admitted, wincing.

"She stopped dead and threw you right over the gate. It took a full minute for the dust to clear from your fall. And what about that time you decided to try bull riding?"

"Another embarrassing failure," she said with a giggle. "But at least I tried. You didn't."

"You were crazy. But I thought you were the most exciting girl I'd ever seen. You were absolutely fearless." He paused, then reached out and touched her face. "What's going on here, Hayley?"

She turned away, staring out at the horizon. "What do you… I don't know what you mean." Was he talking about the kiss? About the attraction that they still obviously felt for each other?

"Look at this place. It's a bloody mess. He's feeding your horse moldy grain. And she doesn't look like she's been exercised or groomed in weeks. Your grandfather used to take such pride in the place."

"I—I didn't know it was getting this bad," she said, grateful that she wouldn't have to analyze the kiss. "I haven't been home for three years. I thought Benny McKenzie was taking care of everything. I was sending money and they were cashing the checks. But then, I spoke to Daisy Willey last week and she told me Benny's mother had taken sick and Benny had left to tend to her. He's been gone a month. But this couldn't have all happened in a month."

"What about the other stockmen?"

"There are no others. My grandfather ran them all off. He thought they were lazy and not worth their pay. And when there was no one left to care for the stock, he sold it. Molly is the last animal on Wallaroo, besides the rabbits and kangaroos and dingoes." She forced a smile. "I'm going to try to convince him to sell the station. Or maybe lease out the land. His health is bad, he's still smoking and he hasn't been to a doctor since I came to live on the station thirteen years ago."

"You're not going to get him off this station," Teague said.

"I have to try," she said, her voice tinged with resignation. "And if I succeed, I want you to take Molly and find her a good home."

Teague nodded. "But until then, I'll bring some decent feed from Kerry Creek when I stop by tomorrow to check on her."

"You're coming back?" Hayley asked, unable to ignore the rush of excitement that made her heart flutter. She'd see him again. And maybe this time, she wouldn't be weeping uncontrollably.

"Follow-up visit," he said. "It's part of the service."

Joy welled up inside her and Hayley couldn't help but smile. Her arrival on Wallaroo had brought nothing but sorrow. And though she knew it would be best to get her grandfather off the station, she'd thought that selling the land would cut her last connection with the boy she'd once loved.

Now that connection was alive again. He was here with her, touching her and kissing her and making her feel as though they might be able to turn back the clock. "Thank you," she said again.

"You need to exercise her," Teague suggested. "Easy at first. A nice gentle walk. You could always ride out to the shack. That's not too far."

Surprised by the suggestion, Hayley couldn't help but wonder if it was an invitation. The shack had been their secret meeting place when they were teenagers. The place where they'd discovered the pleasures of sex.

"Maybe I'll do that."

"I mean, I don't know how long you're planning to stay, but—"

"I don't know, either," Hayley said. "My plans are… flexible. A week or two, at least."

This seemed to make him happy. He looked at his watch. "I really should go. Don't feed her tonight. Just water. I'll see you tomorrow."

She quickly stood up, wanting him to stay but unable to give him a good reason. "Tomorrow," she repeated. Hayley glanced down, wincing inwardly. There were so many things she needed to say, but now didn't seem like the right time. She looked up to find him staring at her. And then, acting purely on impulse, she pushed up onto her toes and kissed his cheek.

She slowly retreated, embarrassed that she'd shown him a hint of the emotions roiling inside her. But then, an instant later, Teague crushed her to his chest, his mouth coming down on hers in a desperate kiss.

In a heartbeat, her body came alive, her pulse quickening and her senses awash with desire. He was so familiar, and yet this was much more powerful than she'd remembered. Her knees wobbled but he was there to hold her.

They stumbled until she was pressed against the rough siding of the stable. His hands drifted lower, cupping her backside and pulling her hips against his. Hayley felt herself losing touch with reality. How many times had she dreamed of this moment? Over the years, she'd wondered what it might be like if they saw each other again. And now, the time had come and she wanted to remember every single second, every wild sensation.

Hayley clutched his shirt, fighting the urge to tear at the buttons. She wanted nothing more than to shed her clothes and allow him to have his way with her. She knew, just by the effects of his kiss, what he could do to her. It had been so long since she'd felt such unbridled passion. Was Teague the man she'd been waiting for all this time?

His palm slid beneath her shirt and up to her bare breast and she arched closer. Cupping her warm flesh, Teague ran his thumb over her nipple until it grew hard. God, it felt so good to have his hands on her body again. All the years between them seemed to drop away and the world was right again.

Hayley worked at the buttons of his shirt and when she pressed her hand against his chest, she could feel his heart pounding in a furious rhythm. "Make love to me," she pleaded.

Her plea seemed to take him by surprise and he stepped back and stared down into her eyes, as if searching for proof that she'd spoken at all. She saw confusion mixed with his desire. Had she made a mistake? Had she moved too fast?

"Hayley! Where are you, girl?"

The sound of her grandfather's voice shocked her

into reality. She quickly straightened her clothes and brushed her hair from her eyes. "Here," she called.

Teague reached for the buttons of his shirt as she turned to wait for her grandfather in the doorway of the stable. "We're watching Molly," she said with a bright smile. "She's better. See?"

He stepped out into the late-afternoon sun, shading his eyes as he searched the paddock. His eyesight had been failing for years, yet he refused to get glasses. Sometimes his stubbornness was downright silly, she mused. At this moment, though, it was convenient. "Where's that damn vet?"

"I'm here, sir."

Hayley steeled herself for what she knew would be a litany of harsh words between them. A Quinn setting foot on Wallaroo was unthinkable. "Grandfather, I don't think—"

"What's your name, boy?" he demanded.

Teague glanced at Hayley, sending her a questioning look and she frowned. Hayley quickly cleared her throat, stunned that her grandfather hadn't recognized Teague. "His name is Tom," she said. "Tom Barrett."

It was the name of one of the characters on *Castle Cove,* but her grandfather had never seen the program so there wasn't much chance of him recognizing the name.

"Dr. Tom Barrett," Teague said, holding out his hand.

"How much is this going to cost me, Dr. Tom Barrett?" her grandfather asked impatiently, ignoring Teague's hand.

"Don't worry, Harry," Hayley replied. "I'll pay for it. Molly is my horse. My responsibility."

"Suit yourself," the old man muttered. He squinted into the sun, then said something under his breath before turning and walking into the barn. Hayley released a tightly held breath. "He didn't recognize you."

"No," Teague said. "Good thing, since he was waiting on the porch with a rifle when I arrived."

She laughed softly, then shook her head. "I knew his eyesight was bad, but not that bad. For a second there, I thought I'd have to break up a fistfight."

"I think I could have taken him," Teague said. He slipped his arm around her waist, pulling her close. "Meet me tonight," he said. "I'll wait for you at the shack."

"I'm not sure I remember how to get there."

"There'll be a moon." He pointed toward the east paddock. "I'll meet you right there at the far gate. Just like we used to. Nine o'clock. We'll ride over together. Molly needs the exercise."

Never mind what Molly needed, she thought to herself. Hayley needed the touch of Teague's hands and the taste of his mouth, the feel of his body against hers. "What if I can't get away?"

"It's all right," he said. "I've been waiting for almost ten years. Another night isn't going to make much difference." With that, he kissed her again, only this time he lingered over her mouth, softly tempting her with his tongue.

A sigh slipped from her lips and Hayley lost herself in the sweet seduction. Every instinct she had cried out to surrender to him, to be completely and utterly uninhibited with her feelings. "Tonight," Hayley said.

He stole one last kiss, then walked backward into the stable, a wide grin on his face. "I sure am glad to see you again, Hayley Fraser."

At that moment, he looked like the boy she'd loved all those years ago. "Stop smiling at me," she shouted, a familiar demand from their younger years.

"Why shouldn't I smile? I like what I see." He picked up his bag and the crate of supplies and continued his halfhearted retreat.

She rubbed her upper arms, her gaze still fixed on his. When he finally disappeared through the door on the opposite end of the stable, Hayley sighed softly. She'd never expected to feel this way again, like a lovesick teenager existing only for the moments she spent with him.

She knew exactly what would happen between them that night and she had no qualms about giving herself to Teague. Of all the men she'd dated, he was the only one she'd ever really loved. And though time and distance had come between them, they were together now. And she was going to take advantage of every moment they had.

2

"WHAT DO YOU WANT to drink?"

Teague glanced up from the plate that Mary had placed in front of him. "Whatever you've got," he replied distractedly. "Beer is good."

She opened the refrigerator and pulled out a bottle, then twisted off the cap with the corner of her apron. Mary had been keeping house at the station for years, hired a few short weeks after Teague's mother had decided that station life was not for her.

He took a long drink of the cold beer, then picked up his fork and dug in to the meal. Dinnertime at the station was determined by the sun. When it set, everyone ate. But Teague had missed the usual stampede of hungry jackaroos tonight. The return trip from Wallaroo had taken longer than he'd planned after he stopped to fix a broken gate.

"Where is everyone?" he asked.

Mary shrugged. "Brody took some dinner out to Payton earlier. And Callum and Gemma disappeared after they helped me with the dishes. They said they were going for a walk." She sat down at the end of the table and picked up her magazine.

"Well?" Teague said. "Aren't you going to offer your opinion? I've met them both and they seem perfectly lovely."

She peered over the top of her magazine. "They add a bit of excitement to life on the station, I'll give them that. At least for Brody and Cal."

Teague chuckled. "Women will do that."

Women could do a lot of things to an unsuspecting man. Since he'd left Hayley at Wallaroo, his thoughts had been focused intently on what had happened between them. He'd replayed all the very best moments in his head, over and over again. The instant that he'd first touched her. The kiss they'd shared. And then the headlong leap into intimacy. His fingers twitched as he thought about the firm warmth of her breast in his palm. "There's nothing wrong with a little excitement every now and then, is there?"

"What about you?" Mary asked, slowly lowering the magazine. "Have you had any excitement in your life lately?"

Teague glanced up. "Excitement?" He chuckled softly. "Are you asking me if I've cleared the cobwebs in the recent past?" Though Mary had served as a mother figure to the three Quinn brothers, she was a bit of a stickybeak, insisting that she know all the relevant facts regarding their personal lives. "Not lately, but I'll let you know if my fortunes change."

She sighed. "I want to see you boys happy and settled."

"Why?" he teased. "So you can get off this godforsaken station and have a life of your own?" Teague watched her smile fade slightly. Mary had always been such a fixture in their lives that they'd hardly considered she might want something beyond her job at the station.

He took another bite of his beef and potatoes, then grabbed a slice of bread and sopped up some of the gravy. "You know, I think it's about time you had a little holiday. I'm going to talk to Callum about it. You could take a week or two and go visit your sister. Or go on a cruise. You could even rent a bungalow on the ocean. Get away from this lot of larrikins."

She shook her head. "There are too many things to be done on the station this time of year. Besides, we have guests. There's not a chance I'd leave those ladies to your care. Now, eat your dinner before it gets cold. My program is on in a few minutes." She stood up and wiped her hands on her apron, then slipped it over her head and hung it across the back of her chair. "Are you going to watch *Castle Cove* with me tonight?"

Teague shook his head. "No, I thought I'd take a ride. There's a full moon and I need to work off some excess energy." He pushed away from the table, then wiped his mouth on his serviette and tossed it beside his plate.

"You barely ate any of your dinner," Mary commented.

"I'm not hungry. Save it for me. I'll eat later." He pulled his saddlebags from the chair next to him, then crossed to the refrigerator. He'd already put the necessities—matches, bottled water, condoms—in the bags. He added a bottle of wine from the fridge and then tossed in a corkscrew from the drawer next to the sink.

He and Hayley had never shared a drink before, but they were old enough now. Maybe she liked wine.

Mary arched an eyebrow. "Do you plan on doing some entertaining tonight?"

"No."

She studied him for a time, then shook her head. "I heard Hayley's back on Wallaroo. But then, I expect you know that already, don't you?"

Teague shrugged, avoiding her glance. "I do. But how did you know?"

"I talked to Daisy Willey today. She called from the library to tell me my books had come in and she mentioned she'd heard Hayley was on her way home. Daisy's cousin, Benny McKenzie, helps take care of the place for old man Fraser, and Benny had to leave to see to his sick mum. So Daisy told Hayley she might want to check up on her grandfather while Benny is gone. Hayley makes a regular donation to the book fund at the library, so she and Daisy keep in touch."

"News travels fast," Teague said.

"Take care," she warned. "You know how your brothers feel about the Frasers. And with the lawsuit heating up again, you don't want to be stuck in the middle. Why Harry Fraser is starting this all over, I don't know."

Teague suspected he knew. If Harry planned to sell Wallaroo, it would be much more valuable with that land attached. "Hayley doesn't have anything to do with that mess," he said. "The land dispute is between Callum and Harry. Besides, I'm a big boy. I know what I'm doing."

"Like that time you did a backflip off the top rail of the stable fence and broke your wrist? As I remember, that was on a dare from Hayley Fraser."

"I'm older now." *But not much wiser,* Teague thought as he slung his saddlebags over his shoulder. He strode to the door and pushed it open, then stepped onto the porch.

He jogged down the steps and headed toward the stables. It was still early and the moon hadn't come up, but he could find his way to the shack blindfolded. When he stepped inside the stable, he flipped on the overhead lights. A noise caught his attention and he squinted to see Callum and Gemma untangling themselves from an embrace.

Gemma tugged at the gaping front of her shirt and Callum pushed her behind him to allow her some privacy. "What are you doing out here?" Callum asked.

"I'm going for a ride." Teague pulled his saddle and blanket from the rack and hauled it toward the paddock door. "Hey there, Gemma."

"Hello, Teague." She peeked around Callum's shoulder and waved. "Nice night for a ride."

He heard Callum mutter something beneath his breath and when he looked back, he saw his brother and Gemma making a quick exit from the stables.

Since the genealogist from Dublin had arrived, Callum had been besotted. Every free moment he could find away from running the station, he spent staring at Gemma. And Brody had brought home a girl of his own, Payton Harwell, a pretty American he'd met in a jail cell in Bilbarra.

Teague threw his saddle over the top of the gate, then whistled for his horse. A few seconds later, Tapper came trotting over, a sturdy chestnut gelding he'd been riding since he'd returned to the station a year ago. He held the horse's bridle as he led it through the gate and into the stable.

It only took a few minutes to saddle his horse and when he was finished, he strapped his bedroll on the back of his saddle, then slipped his saddlebags beneath the bedroll. Every month that he'd been home on Kerry Creek, he'd taken a ride out to the shack. Occasionally, he'd spend the night, sleeping in the same bed where they'd first made love, remembering their sexual curiosity and experimentation.

At least he and Hayley still had a place where they wouldn't be disturbed, a place that would conjure all the best memories. He pulled his horse around and gave it a gentle kick. It had been a long time since he'd felt this optimistic about a woman. And maybe it was silly to think they could return to the way things had been all those years ago. But he hoped they could start over.

As he rode into the darkness, Teague couldn't help but wonder what the night might bring. Would they discuss their past or would they simply live for the moment and be satisfied with that?

HAYLEY STOOD beside Molly, slowly stroking the horse's neck. She'd been waiting in the dark for ten minutes. And for every second of sheer, unadulterated excitement she felt, there was another of paralyzing doubt. Stay, go, wait, escape. She wanted to see Teague again, yet every shred of common sense told her she was setting herself up for heartbreak.

He'd called her fearless. But deep down, Hayley knew that wasn't true. Her childhood bravado had been a way to hide her fears, to divert attention from everything that terrified her. Though she still felt the urge to challenge him, to dare him to prove his devotion to her, she knew better than to risk bodily injury to get his attention, the way she had as a teenager. The only part of her body in peril this time around was her heart.

Over the years, the crazy memories had faded and she'd been left with just Teague, sweet and protective, loyal to a fault. She'd tried to convince herself that they had shared nothing more than a teenage infatuation. They'd discovered sex together and, naturally, there had been a bond between them. But they would have gone their separate ways sooner or later.

Teague had been there to help her through the difficult times. She'd been so confused and angry when she'd arrived on Wallaroo. Her life had been nothing but chaos since the death of her parents, most of the upheaval caused by her rebellious behavior.

Harry had been her only living relative, since her mother was orphaned at a young age, as well. But Harry had refused to take her, and she'd ended up in a series of foster homes. All of them had been fine places, but she'd wanted to be with her grandfather. She'd been constructing a perfect life for the two of them in her mind and was determined to make it happen.

But when he'd finally given in and allowed her to stay at Wallaroo, Harry had wanted nothing to do with her. He was cold and dismissive, barely able to carry on a conversation with her. It had been Teague who had given her a reason to go on with her life, a reason to accept her circumstances and make a place for herself on her grandfather's station—and in Teague's heart.

That's why his desertion had hurt so badly. For months before he'd left for university, she'd tried to tell herself their feelings were strong enough to survive their time apart. And then, after only a few weeks, he'd forgotten her. No letters, no calls. Every letter she'd written had gone unanswered.

Isolated as she was on Wallaroo, she'd assumed the worst of Teague. In the years that had passed after she'd left the station, she'd often wondered what had really happened. Maybe now she would find out the truth.

Hayley had wanted to go to him back then, to demand answers. She'd packed her meager belongings, said goodbye to Molly and hitchhiked as far as Sydney before she ran out of money. After a month there, she'd decided she didn't need anyone to depend upon—or love. She could fend for herself. And in the end, that's where she'd stayed, starting a new life, a life that didn't include anyone who could possibly hurt her.

The sound of an approaching horse caught her attention and she stepped out from behind Molly and peered into the darkness. She held her breath as he came closer, wondering how long it would be before he kissed her again.

Teague maneuvered his horse up next to her, then held out his hand. It had been forever since they'd ridden together. It had been this way when they'd spent nights at the shack. They'd ride out on the same horse, Hayley's body nestled against his so they could talk and touch on the ride home. A few hours before sunrise, Teague would return her to the gate.

He wove Molly's reins through the leather strap on his bedroll, then settled Hayley in front of him. Wrapping his arm around her waist, he gave his horse a gentle kick and they started off at a slow walk.

For a long time, they didn't speak. Hayley felt her heart slamming in her chest and she found it difficult to breathe with Teague so close. She focused her attention on the spot where his arm rested against her belly, shifting back and forth and creating a delicious friction as the horse swayed.

Even after all the time that had passed, this felt safe and comfortable and right. Hayley sighed softly and leaned against him. He nuzzled her neck and she tipped her head to the side to allow him more freedom. His mouth found a bare spot of skin.

Arching against him, Hayley wrapped her arm around his neck, drawing him closer. She was almost afraid to speak for fear she might break the spell that had fallen over her. There was no need to revisit past mistakes and dredge up old resentments. They were here, together, and that was enough.

Teague pressed his palm to her stomach, his fingers splaying across the soft fabric of her T-shirt. But as they continued their silent ride, he slipped his hand beneath her shirt to caress her breast. Hayley inwardly cursed her decision to put on her sexiest underwear. She wanted to feel the warm imprint of his hand on her flesh like she had that afternoon.

The night was chilly and the moon shone golden as it rose over the outback. She had lived so long in Sydney she'd forgotten how desolate it was on Wallaroo—and how incredibly beautiful.

By the time they reached the shack, the silence between them had become part of their growing desire. She didn't need to speak. There'd be time for words later. Teague slid off the horse, then held out his hands for her. Grasping her waist, he held tight as she dropped to the ground. Her breath caught in her throat as he looked down into her eyes. She couldn't read his expression in the dark, but the moonlight outlined his mouth and she fixed her gaze on it, waiting for him to make the first move.

He drew a slow breath, then reached down and ran his fingers through her hair. His lips met hers in a kiss so soft and sweet that it caused a lump in her throat. He took his time, drawing his tongue along the crease of her mouth, teasing until she allowed him to taste more deeply.

Her body pulsed with desire, a current racing through her bloodstream. She shuddered, anticipation nearly overwhelming her.

"Cold?"

Hayley shook her head.

"Scared?"

"Never," she replied, her voice breathless. It was true. She had nothing to fear from Teague. Whatever happened between them, she could handle it.

He took her hand and tucked it inside his jacket, pressing her palm to his chest. "Nervous," he whispered, a smile curling the corners of his mouth.

"It's been a while," she admitted. "For you, too?"

He nodded. Teague took his horse's reins in his other hand and led Hayley toward the shack. He untied Molly's reins and secured both horses to the hitching rail before grabbing his saddlebags. Then he took her hand and they walked up the steps. Hayley paused on the porch. If this shack looked anything like Wallaroo did, she wasn't sure she wanted to go inside.

"It's all right," he said, opening the door.

Hayley waited as he lit an oil lamp. A wavering light filled the shack and she walked inside. Nothing had changed. It was exactly as it had been ten years before. She'd expected cobwebs and dust, but the interior was surprisingly tidy.

"I come out here every now and then and do a bit of housekeeping," Teague said. He set his saddlebags on the small table in the center of the room. "I guess maybe I was hoping I'd find you here one day." He pulled her into his arms. "And here you are."

Teague pushed the door and it swung shut. He slowly drew her jacket down over her arms then tossed it aside. He shrugged out of his own jacket, letting it drop to the rough plank floor behind him.

When he paused, Hayley reached out and began to

unbutton his shirt. She wouldn't be satisfied until they both were naked and lying next to each other in the narrow bed against the wall. As soon as he saw what she wanted, Teague grabbed the hem of his shirt and yanked it over his head.

Hayley's breath froze as she looked at his body in the soft light from the oil lamp. This was no boy. He was Teague, but a different Teague—tall, broad shouldered and finely muscled. Where he'd once had a dusting of hair on his chest, there was now a soft trail from his collarbone to the waistband of his jeans.

Her hand trembled as she smoothed her fingers over his torso. He reached for her T-shirt and pulled it over her head. His gaze immediately dropped to her breasts and he smiled, running his finger beneath the lacy edge of her bra. "Pretty," he said. "I now have hair on my chest and you have expensive underwear."

"I guess we really have grown up," Hayley teased.

Slowly, they continued to undress each other, tossing aside items of clothing one by one. When he was left in his boxers and she in her panties and bra, they stopped. Years ago, she'd always been a bit apprehensive about getting completely naked. It was the only thing that made her feel vulnerable.

But Hayley wasn't a girl anymore. And she wanted to show Teague she was ready to make love to him as a woman, completely free and uninhibited. She reached back and unhooked her bra, then let it slide down her arms. Catching her thumbs in the lacy waistband of her panties, she pulled them down over her hips. Then, without hesitating, she reached over and skimmed his boxers down, his erection springing upright as the waistband passed over his groin.

Hayley straightened and let her eyes drift over his body, taking in all the details. Teague had been a lanky young man, but now he was a fully formed male, with a body that would make any woman weak in the knees.

"God, you are beautiful," he murmured, reaching out to run his hand over her shoulder. "But then, you always were."

"We've both changed," she said.

"One thing hasn't changed," Teague countered. "I still want you as much as I did the first time we made love."

"And I want you," she said.

Teague pulled her against him, soft flesh meeting hard muscle. He was so much taller now, and stronger, and she was surprised by how fiercely he took control. But this was still Teague, still sweet and gentle as he laid her on the bed, then stretched out beside her.

How many times had she fantasized about this? And it had always been the same, the two of them, here in this place, lying naked in each other's arms. Now that her fantasy had come true, she didn't want it to end. Was it possible for the scene to play out again and again, not in her head, but in a brand-new reality?

THE SENSATION OF Hayley's skin meeting his set Teague's desire ablaze. Though he'd often thought back to their times together, he hadn't remembered feeling this incredible. Her skin was silk, her scent like an exotic aphrodisiac. And her body was made to be slowly explored.

Making love with her now would be different from when they were teenagers. They'd both had other partners, and experience was always the best teacher. He stretched out above her, bracing his weight on his hands as he kissed her. But he was like a man parched with thirst. There had been no other women for him, not like Hayley. Desire had been fleeting, something easily satisfied by a one-night stand. But this was much more. As their mouths met again and again, teasing, tasting, he challenged her to surrender.

Her hands smoothed over his face, and every time he drew back, her eyes met his. There was no doubt about what she wanted. Desire suffused her expression, from her damp mouth to her half-closed eyes.

Teague slowly moved his hips and the friction of his cock against her belly sent currents of pleasure shooting through his body. He was hard and ready and longing for the moment when he'd bury himself inside her. But there was no telling how he might react. It felt like the first time, as if every sensation were multiplied a thousand times over. And if he responded as he had that night so long ago, it would be over before it really began.

Her hands drifted down his chest, then grasped his hips, pulling him into each stroke. She moved beneath him, twisting and arching, deliberately taunting him with what she offered. He wanted to take it, right then and there. But Teague fought the impulse and slowly slid down over her body.

The bed was narrow, not made for full-scale seduction. In the end, he knelt beside it, his lips trailing kisses from her belly to her thighs. Everything about her was perfect. This was his Hayley, the girl who had owned his heart for all those years. And yet, she was something more now. She was a woman who had the capacity to break that heart all over again.

Teague didn't care. He didn't care if she disappeared from his life tomorrow. Tonight was all he needed. It was a perfect ending, a way to close the book on all the questions. He would be satisfied and he'd sure as hell make certain she was, too.

Hayley's fingers tangled in his hair as he continued to explore her body with his lips and his tongue. He waited, wanting her to guide him. And when she did, when she drew him to the spot between her legs, Teague didn't hesitate.

He knew exactly how to make a woman writhe with pleasure, how to bring her close to release and then draw her away from the edge. She moaned and whimpered as he took her there, controlling her pleasure with each flick of his tongue.

But Hayley was impatient with the teasing, and every time he slowed his pace, she tightened her grip on his hair. The pain only added to his need to possess her. Teague brought her close one more time, then slid up along her body.

He was breathless now, his need driving him to seek her warmth. She reached down between them to stroke his cock and Teague held his breath, determined to maintain control. He knew he'd have to retrieve a condom, but her touch felt so good that he didn't want her to stop.

She rolled on top of him, her fingers still firmly wrapped around his shaft, then straddled his thighs. Teague watched her as she bent over and placed a kiss on his belly. As she moved up his chest, his fingers tangled in her hair and he relaxed, grateful for the respite.

Yet Hayley wasn't about to stop. She was damp from his tongue and when she shifted above him, he found himself suddenly buried inside her. A tiny gasp slipped from her lips and Teague clutched at her hips, determined to stop her.

He should have known better. When Hayley wanted something, anything, there was nothing that could stand in her way, safety be damned. And it was obvious what she wanted. "Should we stop?" he whispered. "I brought condoms."

"It's all right," she said. "I'm on the pill. And you're the only person I've ever had unprotected sex with."

He smiled. "So are you. We're safe, then."

She didn't answer. Instead, she began to move above him. Hayley braced her hands on his chest, her hair tumbling around her face as she focused on her need. Her eyes were closed and a tiny smile curled the corners of her mouth. Teague watched her, taking in the sheer beauty of her face and body. It was as if she'd been made purely for his eyes. Everything about her was perfect.

Hayley slowed her rhythm, then rose on her knees, until the connection between them was nearly broken.

Then she opened her eyes and moaned as she slowly, exquisitely impaled herself once again. The sensation was more than he could handle and Teague felt himself nearing the edge.

She bent down and kissed him as she repeated the motion. He tried to stop her, holding tight to her hips, but she brushed his hands away, grabbing his wrists and pinning them above his head.

It was no use, Teague mused. She was in control and he had no choice but to enjoy it completely. Her breasts brushed against his chest and he found himself lost in the feeling. He refused to close his eyes, to shut himself off from her beauty.

As Hayley began to increase her rhythm, he knew she was close. He knew her body, her reactions, probably better than she knew herself. He'd taught her how to surrender, how to let go of her inhibitions and fears and experience her first orgasm. The signs were still there— her brow knitted and her bottom lip caught between her teeth.

Teague concentrated on her face, allowing himself to move as she did, closer and closer to the edge. He wanted to share in her release and when the first spasm hit her, he was ready.

She came down on him hard, arching her back as the shudders rocked her body and crying out in pleasure. It came just as quickly to Teague and he grasped her hips as he exploded inside her. He tried to maintain a grip on reality, but the sensation was too overwhelming.

He'd made love to a lot of women since Hayley, but

there was something about being with her that seemed to go beyond mere physical gratification. When he was inside her, he felt a connection deeper than shared pleasure and mutual passion. It was like a silent promise between them, that this intensity, this release, bound them together forever.

It had been nearly ten years since they'd made love, with almost as many lovers in between, but here with her again, time seemed to drop away. He pulled her down beside him and ran his fingers through her hair. Hayley kissed him, still breathless, her face flushed and her lips pliant.

"I guess it's true what they say," she whispered. "It's just like riding a bike. You never forget how to do it."

3

HAYLEY SNUGGLED into the warmth, floating between sleep and consciousness. She opened her eyes, waiting for her vision to clear before completely comprehending where she was.

It all returned to her in a rush, his body, his touch, the feel of Teague moving inside her. And then the overwhelming pleasure of her release. She had wondered what it might be like between them, now that they were both more experienced. But she'd never anticipated the earth-shattering encounter that they'd shared tonight.

How had she ever believed it would just be sex between them? She'd known her desire for Teague was undeniable, something so powerful it had to be satisfied. But she'd been so sure that, once sated, she'd be able to walk away. After all, they no longer loved each other. And without an emotional attachment, sex should be sex and nothing more. That's how she'd approached all the men in her life since Teague—they were useful for physical gratification, but she wasn't interested in emotional attachments.

Yet now that she was here, all she wanted to do was

stay safe in Teague's arms and in his bed. Hayley drew a shaky breath. This was not the smart choice, she reminded herself. It had taken her years to forget him, or at least put him out of her day-to-day thoughts. And now she'd be forced to fight that battle all over again.

It would be so easy to depend upon Teague, to believe that he'd always be there for her. But they lived completely separate lives now, with miles between them, both physically and emotionally. And the only person she could truly depend upon was herself.

Hayley pushed up on her elbow and stared down into his face in the dim light from the lantern. If she concentrated hard enough, she could push aside her memories of the boy she'd loved and see the man capable of breaking her heart. She was stronger now, independent and in charge of her own life. She had a career and plenty of money to assure her security. Everyone told her she had a future in films. There would be no time for a man in her life.

But all the money and fame in the world could never feel like this, Hayley thought—the pure exhilaration and freedom of being herself, the Hayley she'd been before her role on *Castle Cove* had made her a celebrity. She picked up the edge of the blanket and, holding her breath, slipped out of bed.

The early-morning air was chilly against her naked skin as she tiptoed around the shack retrieving her clothes. The sun was already brightening the eastern horizon and if she wasn't back at the house by the time her grandfather got up, he'd come looking for her.

Hayley dressed quietly, watching Teague as she pulled on her clothes and stepped into her boots. She fought the urge to wake him and kiss him goodbye before she left. But she wasn't sure what to say to him. Perhaps it was better to let this settle in before trying to explain it all.

Shrugging into her jacket, she turned for the door. Molly was tied to the rail next to Teague's horse. She unwrapped the reins, then swung up into the saddle, gently wheeling Molly around and pointing her toward Wallaroo.

Hayley drew a deep breath. Though she enjoyed living in Sydney, there were times when she missed the solitude of the outback. The air smelled sweeter and the sun shone brighter on Wallaroo. Though she'd run away from this place, she still considered the station home.

Hayley glanced over her shoulder, taking one last look at the shack, then prodded Molly into a slow gallop. The horse's step was quick and energetic and Hayley was amazed at how Molly's circumstances had changed from the day before. Once again, Teague had been there to save her from certain disaster, to set things right and to make her happy.

Hayley laughed softly. She'd dreaded her visit to Wallaroo. Since she'd first left, she'd only been back twice. But this trip was different. The last two times she'd returned, she had still been so confused and conflicted. This time, she was ready to accept her life as it was. She tipped her face up and whooped as loud as she could, startling Molly.

Teague had promised to return to the station to check

up on Molly and to bring over some fresh feed. She'd
see him again in a few hours and maybe they'd make
plans to spend the night at the shack again. "I can handle
this," she assured herself.

She could, if she managed to maintain a bit of perspective. She wasn't in love with Teague anymore. They
were old friends. Lovers who'd rediscovered each other.
There would be no strings, no serious attachments. And
when it was time to go their separate ways, they would
part without anger or hurt feelings. They weren't teenagers. They were rational, sensible adults.

When she reached the stable, Hayley slid out of the
saddle and held the reins, leading Molly inside. To her
surprise, her grandfather was waiting, sitting on a bale
of hay, smoking a cigarette.

"Where were you?" he demanded.

"I took Molly out for some exercise," Hayley said.
"You shouldn't smoke in here, Harry."

How easy it was for her to lie to her grandfather. And
to divert his attention by changing the subject. She'd
done it throughout her teenage years. But now it bothered her. There was no reason to lie anymore. It was her
right to spend the night with a man if she wanted, even
if that man was Teague Quinn.

"I can smoke any damn place I want to," he said.
"Answer my question."

"I couldn't sleep. I've been worried about Molly all
night. I came out here to check on her and I thought I'd
take her out for some exercise."

He squinted at her, his expression suspicious. "If

you want breakfast, you're going to have to make it," he muttered.

"I'll be in as soon as I get Molly settled. And you don't have to worry about taking care of her. I'll do that from now on."

"I would think so," he said, pushing up to his feet. "She's your damn horse." He walked off toward the far end of the stable with a stoop-shouldered gait.

"Harry, wait a second. I want to talk to you."

"We can talk at breakfast," he called, continuing his retreat.

"No!" Hayley shouted.

Her grandfather froze in his tracks and slowly turned to face her. She prepared herself for his anger, something that she'd become accustomed to in the past. But she wasn't afraid anymore. This man held no power over her. After all this time, she'd resigned herself to the fact that he'd never love her. So what did she have to lose?

"We need to talk," she said in a measured tone as she straightened her spine. "I've noticed your vision isn't what it used to be. I think it's time you go to the eye doctor and get a prescription for glasses. We're not going to argue about this. There's an optometrist that comes out to Bilbarra once a month. I'm going to take you to see him on Thursday."

"There's nothing wrong with my eyes."

"You've been feeding Molly moldy hay. If you couldn't smell it, you should have been able to see it. The station looks bloody awful, the house is a wreck, the yard is all overgrown and you don't see it. I know you wouldn't want Wallaroo to look like this, Harry. But you can't fix what you can't see."

He scowled. "You don't know what you're talking about, girl."

"I have eyes and, unlike you, I *can* see. So, go into the house and get yourself cleaned up and shaved and I'll make breakfast. From now on, I want you to take more care with your appearance. If I have to look at you over the breakfast table then you're at least going to make an effort to look decent. After breakfast, we're going to talk about getting this station back to rights."

Harry thought about her suggestion for a good ten seconds, then, to Hayley's surprise, gave her a curt nod. He turned and shuffled out of the stable, muttering to himself. Hayley smiled. Things had certainly changed. And maybe it wasn't such a long shot trying to convince her grandfather to move off the station. Her powers of persuasion had obviously improved over time.

"The first battle won. Now for the war," she said. She had to be in Sydney by the end of the month, when she'd film her character's return from a short stay in a mental institution, so she didn't have much time. As long as the station wasn't making money, Harry would continue to fall further and further into debt. No doubt her contributions were covering most of his expenses, but she had no idea how he was paying the taxes—if he was paying the taxes.

Though Wallaroo was a small station, just half the size of Kerry Creek, it was worth millions. At least four million, perhaps more. But Harry couldn't spend a dime of it unless he sold the station. He might be able to lease the grazing land, but he'd still be all alone on Wallaroo, without anyone to watch over him. By selling, he'd have enough money to buy a mansion in Sydney and live out the rest of his life in comfort.

And if he lived close by, she could keep on eye on him, make sure he was taking care of himself. After all, for better or for worse, Harry was the only family she had left.

As she tended to Molly, Hayley's mind wandered to thoughts of the man who'd shared her bed the previous night. There had been a time when she'd considered Teague family. When she'd first met him, he'd been like a brother. And then he'd become her best friend. But gradually, her feelings had changed, shifting from affection to sexual attraction.

Hayley smiled, remembering the confusion those emotions had caused. She could recall the exact moment Teague had gone from best mate to object of lust. She'd been fourteen, Teague fifteen, and it had been only days after his mother had left the station with Brody in tow.

She'd found Teague at the rock and he hadn't seemed to be happy to see her. He'd haltingly explained what had happened and Hayley had been surprised to see tears swimming in his eyes. For the first time since her parents had died, she felt the urge to reach out and touch another human being. She'd put her arm around his shoulders to comfort him and then wrapped him in her embrace.

They'd sat that way for a long time and then, when he'd finally gathered the courage to look at her, she'd done something incredibly stupid—or so it had seemed at the time. She leaned forward and kissed him, square on the lips. In the moments after the kiss, her mind had raced for some way to excuse her behavior. But she hadn't needed one. Teague had stared at her as if she'd suddenly sprouted horns and a tail. His face had gone beet red before he'd scrambled off the rock, jumped on his horse and ridden as fast as he could away from her.

Hayley's lips twitched into a smile at the memory. It was at that moment she'd realized her power over him. How something as simple as a touch or a kiss could render a boy speechless. That night, as she'd lain in bed, Hayley had replayed the day's events in her mind. But she'd come away with only one certainty—things had changed between her and Teague Quinn.

From then on, every time she saw Teague, she experienced a physical reaction. Her heart skipped or her stomach fluttered or her cheeks got all warm. That first kiss had led to many more and, eventually, to a slow experimentation in adolescent desire. The relationship had become their little secret, a secret that, if revealed, could bring an end to their time together.

All those silly feelings had come rushing back the moment she'd seen Teague standing outside Molly's stall. But Hayley wouldn't let herself be swept away by emotions this time. Losing her heart to Teague again was not an option. Sexual attraction did not have to include emotional attachment. She'd managed to prove that with the men who'd recently populated her social life. And she'd prove it with Teague.

Hayley took the porch steps two at a time, then

turned and surveyed the yard of Wallaroo station. She had plenty of work to keep her occupied for the next few weeks and plenty to keep her mind off the man who had made her ache with desire the night before. And when she found denial too difficult to bear, they'd meet at the cabin again for another night of unbridled lust.

She smiled as she pulled the screen door open, a delicious shiver racing through her. How long would it be before she saw him again? And what would happen when she did? The answers to those questions were far too intriguing to consider. For now, she'd focus on breakfast.

"Where are you going with that feed? And my ute?"

Teague heaved the bale of hay into the tray of Callum's pickup, then slammed the tailgate shut. "I don't have enough room in the back of my Range Rover. And I'll only be gone a few hours."

"What the hell is going on with you?" Callum asked. "I catch you sneaking in this morning before sunrise and—"

"I wasn't sneaking," Teague said.

"And now you're loading feed into my ute. You could at least tell me where it's going."

"To someone who needs it," Teague muttered. "Charity begins at home." He reached into his back pocket and pulled out his wallet. "All right, how much do I owe you? I'll pay for the bloody feed. I've got three bales of hay, a bag of oats and a bag of the premix."

"You don't have to pay me," Callum said, pushing the

money aside. "Hell, take what you need. I don't care where it's going."

"Thanks, brother," Teague said, patting Callum on the shoulder. "If Doc Daley calls, tell him to ring my satellite phone."

Callum shook his head as Teague hopped into the pickup. If his older brother suspected anything, he wasn't saying, Teague mused. Maybe he didn't really want to know. Callum had inherited their father's distaste for the Frasers and was even crankier now that Hayley's grandfather was making another play for the disputed land.

Of all the Quinns, Teague probably knew Harry Fraser the best, and the old man didn't like to lose, not his money, not his reputation and not his land. Oddly, he didn't seem to care a whole lot about his granddaughter.

Teague turned the ute onto the long, rutted road that led from Kerry Creek to Wallaroo. Though he and Hayley were only a half hour apart over land by horseback, it took a full ten minutes longer than that by road.

As he drove, he picked through his brother's selection of music. Callum had always been a country-music kind of guy, preferring Keith Urban and Alan Jackson. Brody went for hard rock, anything loud and obnoxious. Teague's taste in music leaned toward alternative, little-known bands and singers with interesting lyrics. He managed to find a Springsteen CD in the mix and decided it was the best he'd do. He popped it into the player then sang softly along with the tune.

Just yesterday, he'd taken the same route, his thoughts

filled with memories of Hayley and the time they'd spent together as kids. But now, those thoughts were a pale prelude to what had actually happened between them last night.

He still couldn't believe she was here, within his reach and eager for his touch. She was different, yet she was the same girl he'd fallen in love with all those years ago. The same pale blue eyes, the same honey-colored hair, the same lush mouth and tempting smile.

They hadn't spent much time talking, but there would be time enough for answering all his questions. As he drove, Teague thought about the circumstances that had torn them apart. For months afterward, he'd tried to figure out what he'd done wrong, why it had ended as it had.

But after beating himself up for mistakes he wasn't sure he'd made, Teague realized there had been other forces at work. Maybe her grandfather had driven them apart. Or maybe she'd decided that she didn't love him anymore. Whatever the reason was, he needed to know the real story and Hayley was the only one with the answers.

By the time he reached Wallaroo, Teague had made a mental list of all his questions. He was prepared to take the blame for whatever he'd done wrong and hope that she'd forgive him. As he drove up to the house, he caught sight of her standing on the porch, her hair blowing in the breeze.

The ute skidded to a stop and Teague jumped out, his eyes on Hayley. She hadn't changed in the few hours since he'd seen her last. If anything, she looked more beautiful. Suddenly, all his questions were replaced with an overwhelming need to kiss her. "Hi." The word slipped from his lips like a sigh.

"Hello," she said, a smile playing at her mouth.

Teague took a deep breath and found his voice. "I brought some fresh feed. And I phoned in an order to the feed store in Bilbarra, but they said they wouldn't be able to deliver until later this week. I'll bring more over if you run out."

They stood at a distance, staring at each other, as if afraid to approach. Teague knew that the moment he got within arm's length he'd want to pull her into a long, deep kiss. He glanced around. "Where's Harry?"

"He's inside. I've got him tidying up the house. He's not happy about it, but at least he's not sulking around."

"I'm going to go check on Molly," Teague said, pointing toward the stables. "Do you want to—"

"I'll come with." Hayley bounded down the steps.

He helped her into the ute, then jogged around to the driver's side. As he backed the truck away from the house, Teague glanced over at her, his gaze fixed on her mouth. Kissing her again had become an obsession, something that he couldn't get beyond.

As soon as the truck was far enough from the house, he slammed on the brakes and turned to her. Reaching out, Teague tangled his fingers in the hair at her nape and pulled her toward him. "I missed you," he murmured before bringing his mouth down on hers.

A tiny moan slipped from her lips as he deepened the kiss, his tongue teasing hers. Though the sensation of kissing her was familiar, the passion they'd shared as teenagers was only a fraction of what he felt now. He knew what he could do to her body and what she could do to his.

There was nothing standing in their way now, no silly insecurities or fears of pregnancy. He looked down into her eyes, a frown wrinkling his brow as he thought back to that time. They'd taken a lot of chances when they were younger. Chances that could have changed the courses of both their lives.

"What?" she asked, staring up at him.

Teague shook his head. "Nothing."

She drew a deep breath and forced a smile. "We should check on Molly."

Teague nodded. If they went much further, he'd have to make love to her in the front seat of the ute. Though it might be fun, they certainly could afford to find a more comfortable spot. "How is she doing?" he asked, throwing the pickup into gear and steering toward the stable.

"Good, I think. We had a nice ride back this morning. She doesn't seem to be suffering from any aftereffects of the colic."

"With proper feed, she'll be fine," he said. "And I brought some supplements you can add to her food."

"Thank you. You're a good vet. I knew you would be."

"You always had a lot of faith in me," Teague said, pausing as he stopped the ute at the wide stable doors. "Why didn't you wait?" The question came out before he could stop it. He was afraid to look at her, afraid he'd see anger in her expression.

"I had to get home before Harry woke up," she explained. "And you were sleeping, so—"

"I'm not talking about this morning," Teague said, keeping his eyes fixed straight ahead.

"I—I don't know what you—"

"You know exactly what I mean." He turned to face her, stretching his arm across the back of the seat. "I expected you to be here when I came home. And you were gone. You didn't even bother to let me know where you were."

Hayley stared down at her lap, twisting her fingers together. "I was supposed to wait, I know. And I tried. I was so angry when you left."

"I thought you wanted me to go. You said—"

"What was I supposed to say? I was confused. I thought I could survive alone but as soon as you left, I was…lost. I felt like part of me had been cut away. Once you were gone, there was nothing left for me at Wallaroo, nobody who cared whether I stayed or left."

"But we'd talked about it over and over. I wasn't going to be gone forever. And once you turned eighteen, you could leave on your own and come to Perth."

"My parents were supposed to come home, too, and they never did. I guess I was sure once you left, you'd find someone else, someone smarter, someone prettier. And I didn't want to wait around for that to happen."

"But we made plans, Hayley."

"I know. But the longer you were away, the angrier I got. I wasn't exactly thinking straight. I was confused and scared and a little self-destructive. It's taken three years of therapy to deal with all my rubbish and, believe me, it goes real deep."

"I tried to phone, but Harry wouldn't let me speak to you. And I wrote. Almost every day."

"Harry never told me you'd called, and I never got your letters," she said, frustration filling her voice.

"Would that have made a difference?"

"I don't know. I was in love with you and you left me behind and that's really all I could think about. It was like my parents all over again." She sighed softly. "We can't fix the past, Teague. There's no use talking about it now."

Hayley opened her door and hopped out of the truck. He followed her to where she stood at the tailgate. She picked up a bag of feed and carried it into the stable, and Teague hauled a bale of hay in, as well. An uneasy silence grew between them as he watched her feed Molly.

He sat down on the hay bale, bracing his elbows on his knees, refusing to let the subject die. "Tell me what happened. I mean, I've read the stories in the magazines, about how you were discovered. But tell me."

She stood next to Molly, smoothing her hand along the horse's neck as if it brought her comfort. "I got to Bilbarra hidden in the back of a feed truck. And from there I hitched to Brisbane and then to Sydney. I didn't have any money, so I did odd jobs where I could, mostly washing dishes at restaurants along the way. And then, when I got to Sydney, I found a job at a T-shirt shop on the beach. I lived on the streets and in the parks, in the bus station and the train station. And then one day, this guy walked into the shop and next thing I knew, I was standing in front of a camera, reading lines from a script."

"I came home for semester break and I rode out to

the shack and waited for you. Three days I hung out there. I didn't eat, I didn't sleep. And then Callum told me he'd heard you left Wallaroo two months before. I was…I was scared. Scared I'd never see you again."

"But here I am," she said, glancing over at him.

"That's not what I meant," Teague snapped. She seemed to be so unaffected by what had happened. Surely she must have felt something. She'd walked away from a relationship that had meant the world to him. It wasn't just a teenage crush. He'd loved her. He'd planned his whole life around her. Irritated, Teague stood and strode to the truck, then grabbed another bale of hay.

When he returned to the stall, she was vigorously grooming Molly, wielding the currycomb with careful efficiency. She was angry, too. He knew the signs—the stony silence, the refusal to meet his gaze, the haughty expression.

"I think I have a right to be angry," Teague said.

"I don't know what you want to me to say. I was a kid. I was seventeen. I didn't understand what I was feeling."

"And now?"

Hayley turned to face him, her arms crossed beneath her breasts. "We're both older and wiser. And just because we slept together last night doesn't mean— It doesn't mean anything."

Teague crossed the distance between them. He slipped his hands around her waist and spun her around, pinning her against Molly. His eyes searched her face, then focused on her lips. "I know you, Hayley. Don't forget that. You can't hide from me."

He leaned forward, his mouth hovering over hers, her breath mingling with his. He wanted to kiss her. But he thought better of it. Instead, he let go of her and stepped back. If she was so determined to push him away, then he'd be happy to oblige. "I have to go. I've got calls this afternoon."

"Thanks for the feed," she said.

"No worries."

Teague returned to the ute and dumped the last bale of hay in front of the stable door, then got inside and started the engine. He glanced in the rearview mirror to see Hayley watching him, her chin tilted up in a defensive manner so familiar to him.

She was like one of his wounded birds, so fragile, yet so frantic to escape. He'd been too stupid and naive to see the true depth of her pain when they were younger. But now, he could read it on her face, in the grim set of her mouth and the indecision in her eyes. She was terrified and he knew exactly what was frightening her.

It scared the hell out of him, too—the possibility that what they'd shared all those years ago was real. That the connection between them was still there, as strong as ever. And that she was the only woman he could ever love.

He had his answers now. And yet, Teague found himself plagued with a whole new list of questions.

HAYLEY STARED at the ceiling above her bed, watching a fly crawl across the painted surface. She picked up the script she'd been reading and attempted to finish the page she'd started an hour ago.

The house was silent. Her grandfather usually went to bed immediately after watching the evening news, still keeping stockman's hours even though Wallaroo no longer kept stock. Once the sun went down, there really wasn't much to do…except…

Tossing the script aside, Hayley sat up and brushed her hair out of her eyes. She walked to the bedroom window and looked out into the darkness. It was past ten and the moon hung low in the night sky, softly illuminating the landscape.

Though she and Teague hadn't planned to meet that night, Hayley knew he'd be there waiting. She'd spent the evening devising a litany of excuses not to go to him. Reasons why giving in to her desire was dangerous. But as the night wore on, the reasons became less and less important.

Turning from the window, Hayley retrieved her jeans from a nearby chair. She tugged them on, then stepped into her boots. Her jacket hung on a hook behind the bedroom door. She shrugged into it, buttoning it over her naked breasts, then tiptoed into the hallway.

The stairs squeaked as she made her way down to the kitchen. She slipped out the back door, then ran across the yard toward the stable. Molly's stall was near the door and there was just enough light to see the bridle hanging from the hook on the wall. Hayley grabbed it, went inside and slipped it over the horse's head. But as she reached for the buckle, she felt an arm snake around her waist and lift her off her feet.

She screamed and a hand came down over her mouth.

A moment later, she was outside the stall, twisting against the grasp that held her tight. His grip loosened and she spun around, ready to defend herself. But when his mouth came down on hers, the instinct to fight dissolved, leaving her heart slamming in her chest and her breath coming in shallow gasps.

He didn't say a word and every time she tried to speak, he covered her mouth in another demanding kiss. His palms smoothed over her body, finding bare skin beneath her jacket. Teague turned her around, tucking her against him as kissed her neck.

His touch seemed to be everywhere at once, teasing each nipple to a peak, sliding over her belly, then dipping beneath the waistband of her jeans. He wasn't in any hurry to undress her and in truth, Hayley found the seduction incredibly erotic.

His fingers fumbled with the button at her waist and when it was undone, Teague lowered the zipper. He found the damp spot between her legs and slipped his finger between the soft folds of her sex.

Hayley's breath caught in her throat as desire snaked through her body. Slowly, he caressed her, drawing her closer to the edge while he moved her backside against his hard shaft. They were like teenagers again, too impatient to undress, too desperate to bring each other to release. It was safe, but it was still seduction.

His breath was hot on her neck and she shifted against him, the contact causing a moan to slip from his throat. Hayley wanted to stop, to strip off all their clothes and begin again. But this headlong rush toward completion was impossible to resist.

Her knees grew weak as she lost herself in the pleasure he was providing. Rational thought was replaced by single-minded focus. A burst of sensation spread through her body and then she was there, quivering, waiting, then tumbling over the edge, the spasms too delicious to deny.

She arched back, and his lips found hers, possessing her mouth in the same way he'd taken her body. The orgasm seemed to last forever and Teague wasn't satisfied until she was completely spent and limp in his embrace.

When she could stand on her own again, she turned to face him, ready to return the pleasure that he'd given her. He was still hard, his erection pressing against the faded denim of his jeans. She ran her hand along the length of him and he sucked in a sharp breath.

There were so many ways she could please him, but in the end, she brought him to completion with her fingertips, teasing him, edging him closer and closer, until he came in her hand.

Teague chuckled softly as she continued to stroke him. "The things you do to me," he murmured, nuzzling her neck.

"How long have you been waiting for me?"

"Not long." He brushed her hair away from her temples. "I went out to the shack first and got tired of waiting there. So, I decided to come here and kidnap you out of your bed."

"That would have been exciting," she said. "Although, you may have ended up on the business end of Harry's rifle again."

"It would have been worth it." He looked into her eyes, his features barely visible in the moonlight. "I'm sorry about this afternoon. I shouldn't have gotten angry."

"And I shouldn't have been so irrational. Sometimes, I get a little scared."

"Hayley, you never have to be frightened of me. I would never hurt you."

"You already did," she said. "Once."

"But not deliberately. I was a teenager. I didn't know how you felt. Hell, I couldn't even figure out how I felt. But I think I understand now and I'm sorry I hurt you."

Hayley pushed up on her toes and kissed him softly. "I'm not sure I understand," she said. "But I know we need to be careful. It would be so easy to depend on you again, to feel safe. But I have a life in Sydney and maybe a life in Los Angeles. It wouldn't be a good idea to get all wrapped up in each other."

"Los Angeles?"

Hayley nodded. "My contract with *Castle Cove* is up in September. My agent thinks I could have a career in films, maybe even in Hollywood. He says Australian actresses are hot now. I'm supposed to go there and meet with some casting directors before the end of the month. And he's trying to set up some auditions, as well."

"Los Angeles," Teague repeated. "That's a long way to go for a job. Especially when you have one right here in Australia."

"And the work is good here, don't get me wrong. But if I got a movie, a good movie, then things would change. I'd make more money. My future would be more secure. I wouldn't have to worry. And maybe people would start to see me as a serious actress."

"Is that what you want?"

"I guess. I'm not really qualified to do much else. I didn't go to university. I don't have any other talents or skills. Acting is what I do."

Teague forced a smile. "Then I hope everything works out for you. I mean it, Hayley. I want you to be happy."

"This doesn't mean we can't see each other," she said, reaching up to rest her palm on his cheek. "I just think we should try not to…"

"Fall in love?"

She giggled. Teague didn't mince words. "Yes. Fall in love. I think we should avoid any infatuations. We have to be practical. You have your life and I have mine, and when I leave in a few weeks, everything will return to the way it was."

"But until then, we'll be friends. Friends who might happen to have sex occasionally?"

"Friends with benefits," she said. "I think that's the proper term."

"Ah. So this is a familiar concept to you?"

Hayley shook her head. In truth, she didn't have many friends and certainly no male friends. And the lovers that she'd had were temporary diversions at best. "I've heard it works."

"I'm willing to give it a try."

She held out her hand. "Come with me. I'm sleepy and I want you in my bed."

"Don't you think that's a little risky? With your grandfather in the house?"

"You've slept in my bed before, don't you remember? Two or three times as I recall. The first time was on a dare. You crawled up on the porch roof, then shinnied over to my bedroom window. I'll need to sneak you out before the sun comes up, but we should be safe if you don't act like a yobbo once your clothes come off."

"I can be very quiet," Teague said. "But we're too old to be doing this, Hayley. I don't want to have to watch what I say in bed or sneak out before the sun comes up. If we want to sleep with each other, then we shouldn't need permission."

"We can go back to the shack, then," she suggested.

"That's not exactly five-star accommodations, either," he said. "Hell, I have a plane. We can go anywhere we want."

"No, we can't," she said.

"Why not?"

"Because people recognize me everywhere. Anyone who has a telly knows who I am. My personal life is all over the tabloids. And yours will be, too, if you're seen with me."

"So what do we do?" Teague asked.

"We take what we can get. We ride out to the shack and spend the night together. And in the morning, we go our separate ways."

"Then let's go," he said. "We'll ride out there right now. I want you in my bed tonight."

She wanted to test her resolve, to prove that she could resist if she had to. But in the end, Hayley saddled Molly and they rode out into the moonlight. There'd come a time when she would have to refuse. It wouldn't be tonight. Tonight, she'd give him what he wanted—her body. But she'd take care to keep her heart safe.

4

"DAVEY SAID the colt in the next stall has been sold. He's beautiful."

Teague watched as Payton Harwell tended to his horse, cleaning the gelding's hooves with a pick. Since Payton had arrived on the station a few days before with Teague's younger brother, Brody, the stable had undergone a makeover. The tack room was tidy, the stalls clean, the feed arranged in stacks against the wall. Though Callum hadn't been enthusiastic about hiring the American, Teague could vouch that she knew her way around horses.

She moved with an easy efficiency, feeding and grooming and mucking out the stalls, all in a very orderly fashion. She wasn't afraid to work hard and seemed to enjoy what she was doing, curious about the breeding operation that he oversaw.

"He's going to be trained as a show horse," Teague said. "Some of our horses are used for polocrosse. And some for campdrafting."

At any other point in time, he might have been attracted to Payton. She was smart and beautiful and she seemed to be very well educated. The kind of woman he ought to want. But there was only one woman who captured his imagination these days.

Funny how a few days with Hayley could change his outlook so completely. He found himself anticipating the end of the day, searching for an excuse to see Hayley again. He'd spent the morning and early afternoon making calls, but he didn't intend to spend the evening alone.

Payton set the horse's hoof onto the concrete floor and straightened, brushing her dark hair out of her eyes. "What's that?"

"Besides Aussie rules football, polocrosse and campdrafting are the only native Aussie sports. Polocrosse is a mix of polo and lacrosse and netball. And I reckon campdrafting is kind of like your rodeo riding. The horse and rider cut a calf from the herd, then they have to maneuver it around a series of posts."

"I'd like to see that," she said.

"I'll take you sometime," Teague promised. "There's a campdrafting event in Muttaburra in August if you're still around."

"I'd like to try it."

"Then I'll teach you."

"Teach her what?"

Teague turned to find Brody standing at his side. Though his brother was smiling, Teague sensed an undercurrent of aggravation. Brody was sweet on the new arrival and wasn't doing much to hide his feelings. "Hey, little brother. Where have you been?"

"I went out with Davey to fix the windmill in the high pasture," Brody replied.

"Good to see you putting in an honest day's work," Teague teased, clapping his brother on the shoulder. He smiled at Payton, then tipped his hat. "I've got a call. I'll see you later, Payton. Maybe you can give me a hand tomorrow morning. I've got vaccinations to do on the yearlings."

"Sure," Payton replied. "I'd be happy to help."

He nodded again. "I think I'll like having you here," he said. Teague turned to Brody. "Have you had all your shots?"

Brody's jaw grew tense and Teague decided to make his exit before his little brother decided to reply with an elbow to the nose. Brody had spent five years playing Aussie rules football on a pro team. Aussie rules was a mix of rugby, soccer and professionally sanctioned assault. There was no question who the toughest of the three Quinn brothers was.

"Don't mind Teague," Brody called as Teague strolled out of the stables. "He has a bad habit of yabbering to anyone who'll listen."

Teague pulled off his gloves and shoved them into his jacket pocket, heading toward the house. He had the evening to himself, with only one call on his agenda, a stop at Wallaroo to see Hayley.

Mary was preparing supper in the kitchen when he walked inside. He tossed his hat on the table and washed his hands in the sink.

"Where have you been?" she asked. "Or maybe I needn't bother asking."

Teague put his finger to his lips. "Let's make this our

secret, eh, Mary? I don't need to listen to any whinging from my brothers about my choice of companions."

"I don't think they're in a place to be complaining," Mary said. "They're a bit preoccupied with their own romances."

"I'm heading out," Teague said. "I'm taking my satellite phone, so if Doc Daley calls, tell him to ring me at that number. And I don't plan to be home for a while."

"You haven't slept in your own bed for the past two nights," she said.

Teague grinned. "Yeah. Well, I'm saving you the trouble of making my bed. You should be happy."

Mary shook her head and laughed. "You take care," she said. "I remember what happened the last time that girl broke your heart. You were impossible to live with."

"No one is going to break anyone's heart," Teague reassured her. He pulled open the refrigerator and searched through the contents. "I thought there was another bottle of wine in here."

"Brody took it last night," she said. "Wine consumption has gone up on the station since the ladies arrived." She opened the cabinet above the sink and pulled out a bottle. "Red. It should be served at room temperature."

Teague leaned over and kissed her cheek. "You're a sweetheart, Miss Mary." He strode out of the kitchen onto the back porch, then crossed the yard to his Range Rover. Callum approached from the opposite direction, wiping his hands on a rag as he walked. Teague slipped the wine into his jacket pocket, pushing the neck of the bottle up his sleeve.

"You leaving?" Callum asked.

"Yeah, I've got to drive into Bilbarra to pick up some medicine from Doc Daley."

Callum frowned. "Why don't you take the plane. You should be able to make it home before dark."

Teague shrugged. "I don't mind the drive. I thought I might spend the night. Do a bit of socializing. Since you and Brody have corralled the only two decent-looking women in this part of Queensland, I'm going to have to look elsewhere."

Callum stared at him for a long moment. "You are so full of shit," he muttered. "Who do you think you're fooling? I know Hayley Fraser is on Wallaroo and I suspect you've been seeing her."

"And what if I am?" Teague asked.

Callum shook his head. "Did you ever think that maybe Harry Fraser is using his granddaughter against us?"

Teague laughed. "I think you've got a few kangaroos loose in the top paddock there, Cal. The land is ours. He'll lose, whether I'm seeing Hayley or not. Unless you think he has a valid claim to the land."

"Doesn't matter what I think," Cal said. "Harry's the one raising a stink. He's gone completely round the bend thinking he'll win. This is costing money to defend ourselves once again. I'm ready to sue him right back for the fortune I've spent on solicitors."

Callum had no idea how close he was to the truth

about Harry. He *had* gone a bit berko. And maybe the lawsuit was part of that. "If you must know, Hayley is trying to convince Harry to sell the station."

Callum gasped. "What?"

"He's out there all by himself. He's got no stock, the place is falling down around him and he's probably spending his last cent trying to get that land back. I don't know what good the land will do him, unless he thinks it will raise his asking price for the station."

Callum frowned, shaking his head. "If you really think Harry will sell Wallaroo, you're the crazy one. The only way Fraser is leaving that station is in a casket."

"Hey, I'm just telling you what I know," Teague said as he pulled open the door on the Range Rover. "Hayley is not involved with what her grandfather is doing. She doesn't give a stuff about that land."

As Teague drove the road to Wallaroo, he thought about Cal's attitude toward Harry Fraser. Callum was a reasonable bloke and he always made decisions after careful thought. But his dislike for Hayley's grandfather seemed completely irrational. Yes, the land was valuable. But if the situation were reversed and Callum thought he'd been cheated out of the land, he would do everything he could to get it back.

What difference did it make? Teague mused. He and Hayley were friends. What Callum and Brody thought about their relationship was irrelevant. And if they became more than friends, then he'd have to deal with that when the time came.

When he got to the house on Wallaroo, he found

Harry sitting on the porch, his feet resting on the railing, his hands folded over his stomach. He sat up straight as Teague leaned out of the window of the Range Rover. "Hello, Mr. Fraser."

"She's in the stables. If you're here to collect on your bill, she's going to pay it. It's her horse."

"No worries," Teague said. "I'm sure she's good for it."

"If you're not back for money, what are you doing here?"

"Just another follow-up call," Teague said.

"Get on with it, then," he said, calling an end to their conversation.

By the time Teague reached the stables, Hayley was headed toward the house. He pulled up beside her and reached out, smoothing his hand along her bare arm. "Get in," he said.

"Where are we going?"

"Out," Teague replied.

"There is no out in the outback. We're already out."

"Well, I have a destination in mind. We'll have a little wine, maybe a bite to eat. After that, maybe we'll see a show." He reached over and opened the passenger-side door. "Come on. We're going to be late."

She gave him a dubious look, but hurried around the SUV and jumped inside. Instead of driving toward the road, Teague drove through the yard and past the stables. The Range Rover bumped along toward the sunset, dust billowing behind them. Teague had seen the landing strip from the air the last time he'd passed over Wallaroo and he wanted to see it up close. When he reached the long, flat stretch, he turned the SUV around, its tailgate facing west.

"What are we doing out here?" Hayley asked.

"The best show in all of Queensland," Teague said as he helped her out. He pointed to the brilliant pinks and purples on the horizon. "We're just in time." Teague opened the tailgate of the Range Rover, then lifted Hayley up to sit on it. Then he retrieved the bottle of wine from behind the driver's seat. "And I brought refreshments."

Hayley smiled. "Is this a date? Are you trying to impress me?"

"Is it working?" Teague asked.

"Yes."

"Then this is a date," he said. He took a corkscrew out of his pocket and opened the wine. "I didn't bring glasses. We'll have to drink out of the bottle."

"It's so much more sophisticated that way," Hayley teased. "That's the way they do it at all the best restaurants in Sydney." She crossed her legs in front of her. "You know, this is our first date. In all the time we knew each other as kids, we never went on a real date. No school dances, no parties. I wish we would have had something like that to remember."

"We'll have this," Teague said.

"Maybe we shouldn't." Hayley sent him a sideways glance. "Maybe we're getting ahead of ourselves. We're so anxious to rekindle a teenage romance that we aren't thinking about the effect it will have on our lives."

"Are you saying you don't want to be with me?" Teague asked.

"No. I'm saying, when this is over, I might not be able to cope with losing you again. I feel happy when I'm with you, Teague. The world seems right."

"You'll always have me," he said. "You don't have to worry over that."

She took a sip of wine, then smiled ruefully. "We'll be eighty years old and I'll show up on your doorstep wondering if our 'friends with benefits' deal is still good."

"And I'll invite you in for a cup of tea and a Vegemite sandwich and we'll watch a nice game show on the telly." He bumped her shoulder with his. "And you'll be wearing some of those sexy stockings that end at the knees and comfortable shoes and a nice hairnet and I won't be able to keep my hands to myself."

"Now you're making me really depressed," she said.

Teague took the wine and set it down beside her. Then he leaned forward and dropped a kiss on her damp lips. "I can make you feel better," he offered. "It's the perfect remedy. Have you ever had sex on the roof of a Range Rover at sunset?"

"I can't say that I have," Hayley answered.

Teague reached into the rear of the SUV and pulled out a blanket, then tossed it over his head. He stood up on the tailgate and pulled her up to her feet. Spanning her waist with his hands, Teague lifted her up to sit on the roof, then handed her the bottle of wine.

"I knew there was a reason I didn't get the optional roof rack," he said as he crawled up beside her. "Sweetheart, you are never going to forget our first date."

A MANTLE OF STARS filled the inky sky. Away from the lights of the city, Hayley was amazed at the sight, like a million diamonds scattered above her. Only in the outback, she mused. Snuggling against Teague, she sought the warmth of his body to ward off the chill of the night air. They lay facing each other, the blanket wrapped around them both, their noses touching.

"This was the nicest first date I've ever been on," she teased, her lips brushing against his as she spoke.

"I know what a woman likes," he said. "I'm pretty smooth that way. Wine directly out of the bottle, a beautiful sunset and really incredible sex on the roof of my car."

"So, how many other women have you had since me?"

"I don't remember," he said.

Hayley drew back. "You're lying."

"I'm saying that none of them were memorable. You were the one who stuck in my mind. I think I can recall every single time we made love." His hand ran up along her hip, then down again. "Would you like me to recall them all for you?"

Hayley shivered, nuzzling against his neck. "I guess it's true what they say. You never really forget your first love."

"Very true," he agreed.

"We should probably go. Harry is going to wonder where I am."

"It's not that late. We can stay a bit longer." He kissed her again, this time lingering over her lips. "I want to say something to you and I want you to listen carefully."

"What is it?" Hayley asked, wondering at his serious tone.

"I plan to spend as much time as possible with you, Hayley. I don't know how long you'll be here, but I'm determined to make every minute count. So when we're together, there'll be no talk of getting home or worrying about Harry or maybe we shouldn't be doing this or that. If you're not prepared to spend every free minute with me, you need to tell me now."

"You have to work," she said.

"I do. But I figure you can come along. That's why I wanted to check out the landing strip. I'll buzz the house and you can meet me out here and off we'll go. What are you doing tomorrow? I have to fly into Bilbarra to cover a couple surgeries for Doc Daley. After we're done we can fly to Brisbane for lunch."

"I have to take Harry into Bilbarra. The eye doctor stops there tomorrow and he has an appointment to get his vision checked. We're leaving first thing in the morning. Two hours in the car on the way to Bilbarra and two hours back. I'm not sure how that's going to go."

"Why don't you let me fly you both. It's about a half hour by air. Once I'm finished at the surgery, we'll have lunch."

"Harry would never get on a plane," she said. "I'm going to have the devil of a time getting him in my car. He's very suspicious of everything I suggest to him. He'll probably think I'm planning to dump him off at some retirement home."

"He must leave the station occasionally. Doesn't he?"

"From what I can tell, not recently. He'd been living off tinned food for a month before I arrived. This station was his whole life. It's kind of sad to see what's happened to it. Makes the feud seem a bit silly, doesn't it?"

"Why is he bringing this up again? He's lost the last two times in court. And the time before that, he only won because he found some old document that the judge thought was real."

"I don't know," Hayley replied. "He has no money to pay for this lawsuit. He's not using the land he has. He's so fixated on winning." She drew a deep breath. "Couldn't you let him win?"

Teague frowned. "You mean turn over the land to Harry? Cal would never go for that."

She nodded. "Why not? I'm beginning to think the feud is the only thing keeping my grandfather on this land. He simply refuses to leave until he wins."

"He's not going to win this time," Teague said.

"What if I bought the land from Cal? How much would your brother want for it?"

"He won't sell," Teague said. "Why do you care? Harry never did anything for you except drive you away from the only home you had left. You don't owe him anything, Hayley."

"You don't understand," she countered.

"Explain," he said. "Make me understand."

Teague waited, watching as she tried to put her thoughts in order. "You're right, I don't owe Harry anything. But he's the only family I have. And I can't continue to push him away. There's going to come a day when he isn't around anymore and I don't want to have any regrets about what I did or didn't do."

Teague caught her hand and drew it to his lips. "You can't make him love you. Even if you handed him that land on a silver platter, it wouldn't change who he is."

"I know." She drew a ragged breath. "He seems so old. And sad. And when he's gone, I won't have anyone left."

"You'll have me," he said in a fierce tone. "How many times do I have to say that for you to believe it?"

"Kiss me again," she said. "Then maybe I'll believe it."

Teague cupped her face in his hands and kissed her softly. Tears pushed at the corners of her eyes and she fought against them. She never cried. She hadn't cried since her parents' funeral. And now, twice in one week. Teague was the dearest friend she'd ever had, the only person in the world she could trust. Yet, she couldn't allow herself to surrender to those feelings.

He pulled away and Hayley swallowed the lump in her throat. Before he had the chance to see her tears, she rolled over on top of him, pushing the blankets aside. Goose bumps prickled her skin as the chilly night air stole the warmth from her body. She ran her fingers down his chest from his collarbone to his belly.

The cold magnified every sensation, the simplest touch warming her blood and making her heart race. Teague smoothed his thumb over her nipple and Hayley sighed softly, bracing her hands on his chest.

She moved above him, teasing at him until he began to grow hard with desire. And when he was ready, Hayley shifted and he was suddenly inside her. She moaned as he thrust deep, his hands clutching her hips.

She could lose herself in this passion. When he was

inside her, all her doubts and insecurities vanished. The connection became strong and the trust unshakable. But they couldn't spend the rest of their lives making love. They both had to live in the outside world, where other forces would pull them apart.

If only she knew what to do, how to commit to a man. Without an example to follow, without loving parents to watch, she'd been left to find guidance from romantic movies. But that wasn't real life.

Her parents had loved each other, against all odds. They'd met and fallen in love in the course of a day, then married young, just a year after her father had left Wallaroo. They'd started with nothing and built a life together. But how did it happen? She'd been too young to see the truth in their relationship. To her, they'd seemed perfect. Yet they must have had their problems just like any other couple.

Had it begun like this? Hayley wondered. With desire and passion and need? Or was there some other secret to making love last a lifetime? She looked down at Teague, his face cast in silver light from the moon, then bent closer and kissed him.

He twisted his fingers through her hair, holding her close, whispering his need against her mouth. Then he reached between them and touched her. She drew in a quick breath, then moaned, an unspoken plea for him to continue.

Hayley gave herself over to him, light-headed with desire and unable to think rationally. It felt so good to let go, to know that he would be there to catch her when she fell. She could allow herself to be vulnerable without the usual fears.

The seduction was slow and deliberate, a gentle climb toward release. And when it finally came, she and Teague found it together, their bodies joined in perfect pleasure. Hayley didn't know much about love, but she knew what they shared sexually was as good as it got.

He pulled her into his embrace again, tucking her against his warm body and wrapping the blanket around them. "We can't go on like this," he murmured.

"We can't?"

"I don't want to leave you. I want you with me."

"That's not very practical," she said.

"I'll find a way to make it happen. Twenty-four hours together with no one to get between us. Two days would be even better."

"I'm cold," Hayley said, anxious to change the subject.

"I think I'm going to have to find our clothes." Teague wrapped her up in the blanket, then slid off the top of the Range Rover.

She sat up and watched him, appreciating his body naked in the moonlight. He gathered his clothes first, pulling his shirt over his head before he tugged on his jeans. Then he searched for his boots and socks. When he was finished dressing, he returned with her clothes.

"So, tomorrow you have to take Harry into Bilbarra. I'll drive you. I'll be here at seven sharp. You can take care of your business in town while I stop at the surgery. We'll drive home in the afternoon and then spend the night at the shack."

"I don't think this is a good idea. A Quinn and a Fraser in the car together for four hours."

"Dr. Tom Barrett will be taking you to Bilbarra. Your grandfather loves me. I'm the one who saved your horse, remember? And I gave you a discount on the bill."

"You didn't charge me anything," Hayley said as Teague pulled her T-shirt down over her head.

He helped her find the sleeves, then gave her a quick kiss. "I prefer to get compensated in other ways."

"Where are my panties?" she asked, searching through the pile of clothes.

"I think a dingo ran off with them."

"This is awful. I lose my panties on our first date."

"I can hardly wait for the second date." Teague winked at her.

"Don't be so certain. Harry will be coming along tomorrow."

"Maybe I can find *him* a date," Teague joked.

TEAGUE FIXED HIS GAZE on the road in front of him. He fought the temptation to glance at the clock on the dashboard. No matter how much he wanted this day to be over, counting down the minutes wouldn't make it go any faster.

"Have you seen the horses they breed?" Harry asked. "Scrawny creatures. A wonder they manage to sell even one. But then, the Quinns have always been cheats— every last one of them."

Teague gritted his teeth. His jaw was beginning to ache with the effort to remain silent. He'd listened to

Harry blathering all the way to Bilbarra. The old man seemed determined to offload every imagined insult and slight that the Quinn family had ever perpetrated against him. Teague was beginning to wonder if Harry knew who he really was and was provoking him deliberately. Likening Teague and his brothers to con men was over the top.

Hayley sent him an apologetic smile. "How are your new glasses working, Harry?"

"I don't need glasses."

"Put them on. You won't get used to them if you don't wear them."

"They make me look like a fool," he muttered.

"They make you look very clever," Hayley countered.

"What would you know, girl?"

"Don't speak to her like that," Teague said, staring at Harry in the rearview mirror. "She doesn't deserve that."

"What do you know about what she deserves?" Harry snapped.

With a low curse, Teague slammed on the brakes. The Range Rover skidded to a stop and Teague twisted around to face Harry. But Hayley put her hand over his. "Nature break!" she said, sending him a warning look.

She jumped out of the SUV and ran around to Teague's door. "Come on," she said, yanking the door open and grabbing his hand. "I want you to watch for snakes."

They walked into the brush, Hayley clutching his hand and tugging him along behind her. "What are you doing?"

"What am I doing? What is *he* doing?"

"He's being Harry. That's the way he is."

"He's rude. And he treats you like crap. I'm not going to listen to him speak to you like that. I won't have it, Hayley."

"It's just the way he is," she said. "It doesn't bother me. I've learned to tune it out."

"Well, you shouldn't have to." He braced his hands on his hips and shook his head. "You're not staying on Wallaroo any longer. You're coming to Kerry Creek with me."

"What?"

"I won't allow you to be subjected to his tantrums. And you wonder why you're carrying around so much baggage? Well, there's one big windbag you can get rid of right now."

"He's family," she said. "You don't have any idea what it's like to have no one. You have two parents and two brothers. I have him. And yes, he can be a pain in the arse at times, but he's still my grandfather."

"He's also the guy you ran away from ten years ago. And the guy who refused to take you in right after your parents died."

"Well, I've had time to realize my mistakes," she said. "And now, I'm waiting for him to realize his."

"Why is it so important? He'll never be what you want, Hayley."

"I'm not going to argue about this," she said, turning to walk away from him. "Not here."

Teague followed her, grabbing her arm and spinning her around to face him. "We're not getting in that car until you agree to come to Kerry Creek and stay with me."

"Then we're going to be out here all day and night, because I'm not going to Kerry Creek. Do you think I'll be any more welcome under your brother's roof than I am under my own?"

"You won't even give *us* a chance, will you?"

"What is that supposed to mean? What do *we* have to do with me coming to Kerry Creek?"

"No matter what I do, you're never going to need me. You're too scared to need anyone, Hayley. That's why you ran all those years ago. And that's why you're still running right now."

"Don't try to analyze me. You're no good at it."

"I know you better than anyone in this world."

"You used to know me," she said. Hayley turned and walked toward the road. She got inside the Range Rover and slammed the door behind her.

Teague cursed, then kicked the dusty ground in front of him. Hayley was the most beautiful woman in the world, but there were times when he wondered what the hell he was doing with her. She stubbornly refused to acknowledge she might deserve a bit of happiness in her life. The closer he tried to get, the more she pushed him away.

Last night, under the stars, he'd felt as if they'd finally gotten past her insecurities. But then, hours later, she'd found a way to sabotage what they'd shared. They were running around in circles and he was getting dizzy.

Teague walked back to the SUV and got inside. He threw the car into gear and pulled out onto the road. The problem was he and Hayley would never get things right between them if there was always someone standing in the way. His brother, her grandfather and Hayley herself.

He glanced over at her and found her staring out the passenger-side window. Maybe trying to reestablish a relationship with Hayley wasn't worth the trouble, Teague mused. They'd be going their separate ways in a few weeks. The more time they spent together, the more they seemed to be at odds with each other.

The rest of the ride passed in silence. When Harry made a move to speak again, Hayley quickly shut him down. To Teague's surprise, the old man followed her order, slumping in the rear seat with his arms crossed over his chest. He'd seen that posture from Hayley too many times. Maybe they were closer than he'd thought.

When they reached Wallaroo, Teague pulled up in front of the house. Harry shoved his new glasses onto his nose and peered out the window. "Jaysus," he muttered. "That house needs to be painted." He got out of the SUV and walked up to the porch, examining the peeling paint, then disappeared around the corner of the house.

"Come home with me," Teague said.

"I can't. Thanks for the ride. I know he can be a horror sometimes. But I can handle him now. He doesn't bother me."

"You deserve better."

She forced a smile, then nodded silently. A moment later, Hayley jumped out of the truck and closed the door. She gave him a little wave, before turning and running into the house.

As the Range Rover bumped down the road, Teague tried to put the day in perspective. Life couldn't always be perfect. They weren't kids anymore and there would be differences between them. But he knew more now than he had ten years ago. It wasn't easy to fall in love or to stay in love. Sometimes the differences between two people were too large to overcome.

There was an upside to staying away from Hayley. He wouldn't have to think about her 24/7. He could get his work done without having to hurry home so he might spend the night with her. And he and Callum would be on better terms.

So that was it. He'd given seeing Hayley a go and it hadn't worked. "Nothing ventured, nothing gained," he muttered to himself. Would she be that easy to give up? Though it would be a challenge to stay away from her, he was determined to try. He had calls to make tomorrow and the next day, he'd promised to fly Gemma and Payton to Brisbane so they could do some shopping.

He wouldn't have time to even think about Hayley until Sunday. By then, maybe he'd be ready to forget her and go on as if nothing had happened between them. "Right," he said, knowing that was all but impossible. His attempts to stop thinking about Hayley would only lead to more thoughts about her.

All the way home to Kerry Creek, Teague tried to figure out a way around the walls Hayley had constructed. If anyone could breach them, he could. But as he was furiously taking them apart, brick by brick, she was frantically building them thicker on the other side.

It was her move, Teague decided. He would wait for her to come to him. She couldn't run away if he refused to chase her.

When Teague got to the station, he didn't bother stopping at the house. Instead, he drove directly to the landing strip. He had a few hours left until sunset. If he stayed on the station, he'd only be tempted to ride out to the shack. He'd have to put some space between himself and Hayley.

He'd fly back to Bilbarra. Once the sun went down, he couldn't land on the station. He'd be stuck where he was. He'd spend the evening getting pissed at the Spotted Dog, sleep it off on Doc Daley's office sofa and then make his calls tomorrow.

It was a decent scheme, with no room to make a fool of himself. And that's all he really wanted from here on out—to keep from playing the fool.

5

HAYLEY WOVE Molly's reins through her gloved fingers, then turned the horse away from the stables. With a gentle kick, she urged her into a slow gallop. The early-morning air was chilly, the breeze whipping at her hair. But a ride was exactly what she needed.

She'd spent the last two nights wide-awake, fighting the temptation to ride out to the shack and see if Teague was waiting for her. Her therapist would probably say she was reverting to the self-destructive patterns of her childhood, making a bad decision simply to punish herself. But Hayley knew it was something more than that.

Was she trying to test him? To see how deep his affection ran? Or was she trying to drive him away before he had a chance to leave on his own?

Her stomach fluttered as she thought about what she'd say if he was waiting for her. She managed to stay away from the shack partly because of the fear that he might not be there. If he wasn't there then he didn't care and it was all over. She'd half expected him to stop by the station with the excuse of checking up on Molly, even though the horse had recovered completely. And he hadn't come. In two days, no word from the only person in the world who claimed to care for her.

She urged Molly to gallop faster and faster. Hayley's legs ached and her breath came in shallow gasps, but she didn't want to stop. As she came over a small rise, she saw the shack in the distance. Two horses were tethered out front.

Drawing a deep breath, she headed toward the shack. Had he been there all night waiting? When she reached the porch, Hayley slid out of the saddle and dropped softly to the ground. She walked up the steps, then rested her hand on the doorknob. As she opened it, the hinges creaked. "Teague?"

Hayley froze as she saw the two naked bodies intertwined on the small bed. She felt her world shift, the ground moving under her feet. Teague had brought another woman to their special place. How could he have done this? Was he trying to punish her?

With a soft sob, Hayley turned and ran down the steps. She heard a voice call out behind her, but her heart was beating so hard and fast that it obliterated every sound around her.

She fumbled to put her foot in the stirrup, frantic to escape before he discovered her here. She swung her leg up and over the saddle, then reached for the reins.

"Wait!"

Hayley glanced up, tears swimming in her eyes. Slowly, she realized the man who stood on the porch wasn't Teague at all. Though the family resemblance was obvious, she found herself looking at a man who could only be Teague's younger brother, Brody. She'd only seen him once, when he was much younger, but she knew it was him.

"What are you doing here?" she demanded, her voice shaky and her hands trembling.

"We needed a place to sleep," Brody explained. "This was close by. Was Teague supposed to meet you here?"

"No," she snapped, keeping a tenuous hold on her emotions. "Why would you think that?"

He shrugged, then shoved his hands in his jeans pockets. "It was almost as if you were expecting him," Brody said, his eyebrow arched.

Hayley swallowed hard and tried to steady her voice. "I saw the Kerry Creek horses and I thought it might be him. But I was mistaken. Sorry. I didn't mean to wake you."

"Should I tell Teague you were looking for him?" Brody asked.

"Why?" Hayley shook her head, unwilling to reveal her true feelings to Teague's brother. "No. You don't need to tell him anything."

A moment later, a woman joined Brody on the porch, her eyes sleepy and her long mahogany hair loose around her shoulders. He turned to her and smiled, slipping his arm around her shoulders. "Morning," she said, nodding to Hayley.

"Payton, this is Hayley Fraser," Brody said. "Her family owns this place. Hayley, Payton Harwell."

Payton smiled warmly. "Thank you for letting us

stay here. I got lost last night and wasn't really prepared to sleep outside."

Hayley nodded, still suspicious of Brody's friendly attitude. She knew what Teague's brothers thought of her, what his whole family thought. She was trouble, a girl who didn't deserve a brilliant boy like Teague. His parents had tried to put an end to their friendship early on and when Teague had been forbidden to see her, they'd simply snuck around, taking whatever time they could find together.

"I—I have to go," Hayley said. "Stay as long as you like. I won't say anything to my grandfather."

Hayley couldn't contain her humiliation as she rode back to the house. Once again, tears flooded her eyes and she brushed them away with her fingers. What was wrong with her? She'd never been this emotional before. This was what romance did to her—it caused her heartache and pain.

But mixed with the humiliation was a large dose of frustration. She'd been the one to mess everything up. Teague had done nothing but offer her his friendship and affection and she'd thrown it in his face. He was right. She didn't owe anything to Harry. If it came down to a choice between Teague and her grandfather, she should have chosen Teague.

Harry may be family, but Teague was something more. Teague was a true friend. Hayley sighed. No, he was more than a friend. A lover. "A lover that I don't love." She groaned. A soul mate? Was that it? The notion seemed so sentimental, but it came the closest to de-scribing how she felt.

There was no one in the world she trusted more. Considering she usually trusted no one but herself, that was saying a lot. And there wasn't one other man with whom she'd rather spend an evening. He knew what she was thinking before she said it, as if he could see right into her mind. And Hayley was certain that no matter how much time had passed, she could depend on him if she needed help.

As she approached the stable, Hayley noticed Teague's truck parked nearby. Her heart leaped and she kicked Molly into a quicker pace. When she got inside the stable, she saw him sitting on a bale of straw at the far end. He glanced up at the sound of Molly's hooves on the concrete and then got to his feet.

Hayley jumped to the ground and took a step toward him. For a long moment, they stared at each other, and then a tiny sob racked her body and Hayley ran toward him. Teague gathered her in his arms, lifting her off her feet as he kissed her.

"I'm sorry. I'm sorry," he whispered between kisses.

"No, I'm sorry," Hayley said. "I was such a bitch to you. And you didn't deserve that."

"I need to be more patient," he said, setting her on the ground. He held her face in his hands and kissed her again. "I've been miserable these last few days. All I could think about was you. I was in Brisbane yesterday and I was walking through David Jones and everything I saw reminded me of you. I wanted you there with me."

"You went shopping to get your mind off me?"

Hayley asked. "Don't men usually go to a pub and get themselves drunk?"

"I did that on Thursday night. Saturday I took Gemma and Payton shopping in Brisbane."

"I met Payton," she said softly. "I rode out to the shack this morning and she was there with Brody."

"So that's where they ended up," Teague said with a soft chuckle. "I guess that's not our private place anymore."

"She seemed nice," Hayley said. "Very pretty."

"I've never known Brody to be this far gone for a girl before and he's had lots of girls. And Cal, he's got a sweetheart, too. Though I'm not sure he knows what the hell to do with her. Her name is Gemma and she's a genealogist from Ireland. Things have changed at Kerry Creek in the past week."

"Is that why you asked me to come and live with you? So you'd have someone there, too?"

"No. And I shouldn't have asked. I know how you feel, and Cal and Brody haven't ever done anything to get to know you better. But that's going to change."

"How? Are you going to beat them up if they say anything nasty about me?"

"Yes," Teague said, nodding his head. "I will thoroughly thrash them to defend your honor. But before I do, I'm going to give them a chance to get to know you. I want you to come to Kerry Creek tomorrow. We're having a little celebration for the queen's birthday, a barbecue. And I'm inviting you to be my guest."

"I don't know, Teague. If I come, Callum and Brody will be upset and I'll ruin everyone's good time."

"But if you don't come, you'll ruin my good time," he said. Teague slowly rubbed her arms, searching her gaze until she couldn't help but smile at him. "It will be fun. We're going to have games and a campdrafting competition. It will give you a chance to show off your skills on a horse. And you can see Payton and meet Gemma and talk about…girl stuff."

In truth, Hayley would have been happy to avoid Callum and Brody for as long as she could. But Brody had been rather nice to her at the shack. Maybe their feelings had softened a bit now that they were older. "All right. I'll come, but if your brothers don't want me there, then I'm going home."

"I'll pick you up at—"

"No, I'll ride over," Hayley said. "In case I decide to leave early."

"You won't want to leave." He kissed her again. "I promise. You'll have a good time. Now, I have the day off. What are we going to do with ourselves?"

"We could go riding," Hayley said.

"We could fly to Brisbane to see a movie," Teague suggested.

"We could drive to Bilbarra and have lunch at Shelly's."

Teague bent close, his forehead pressed to hers. "Or we could ride out to the shack, kick Brody and Payton out and spend the rest of the day in bed."

"I vote for the shack," she said.

"Me, too."

He walked over to Molly, who had been munching on some loose hay in her stall, and led her to the door.

He swung up into the saddle, then shifted to make room for Hayley. He held out his hand and pulled her up to sit in front of him, then clucked his tongue.

Hayley settled against him, holding tight to the arm he'd wrapped around her waist. Everything was all right now. She hadn't made a mess of things. Teague still cared and she had another chance to show him how much he meant to her.

"I'LL GIVE YOU THIS," Brody said. "She's not hard to look at. I've watched her program a few times with Mary. They make her look like a real tart on the telly. She looks much better in person."

"They say the camera adds ten pounds," Callum said soberly.

"Who says that?" Teague asked, laughing at his brother's comment.

Callum shrugged. "I don't know. They. People who know that kind of shit. I'm not saying she's fat, because she isn't. And I think she's pretty enough, but Gemma is much prettier."

"Payton has them both beat. Dark-haired girls are always more attractive," Brody said. He nodded in the girls' direction. "What do you suppose they're talking about?"

The three women were standing along the far fence, their arms braced on the top railing as they chatted. The conversation must be going well, Teague mused, because Hayley was smiling.

Callum folded his hands over his saddle horn. "I

don't know. Maybe recipes. That's probably it. They're exchanging recipes."

This time both Brody and Teague laughed. "You don't know anything about women, Cal," Brody said. "They're probably talking about shoes or clothes."

"Or they could be talking about us," Teague offered. "The same way we're talking about them."

"What? Like they're discussing how pretty we are?" Brody asked. "There's not much to discuss. I'm a better-looking bloke than the two of you. End of story."

"Brody has always been the pretty one in the family," Callum said. "We've always thought of him as our little sister, haven't we, Teague?"

"And since you're the one with all the experience around women, little sis, you go over there and find out what they're talking about," Teague suggested.

"I'd guess they're probably talking about what a pair of dills you two are," Brody muttered as he rode away.

"You're not upset that I brought her here, are you?" Teague asked.

"No," Callum said. "My fight is with Harry Fraser, not his granddaughter. Besides, you could always marry her and then Wallaroo would be yours someday."

"What the devil are you talking about?"

Callum gave him a dubious look. "Don't tell me you haven't thought about it. She'll inherit. Harry doesn't have any other heirs. Though Wallaroo is smaller than Kerry Creek, it has some prime grazing land. And it would be the perfect place to raise horses. You've always wanted to do that. Isn't that why you went to vet school?"

"I told you, Hayley isn't interested in the station. She's going to try to convince Harry to sell it."

"You should talk her out of that," he said. "That land is worth a whole lot more than what anyone will pay for it now, especially since it borders Kerry Creek."

"You could always buy it," Teague said.

"Yeah. If three or four million dollars falls out of the sky tomorrow, I could. But I'm not holding my breath on that one."

They watched as the ladies climbed over the fence and walked across the yard toward them. Brody had talked them into taking part in the campdrafting competition. They'd compete as pairs against each other.

Though Callum was the best at driving cattle, it was obvious Gemma wasn't comfortable around horses. Payton, however, was an experienced horsewoman, but she'd never attempted campdrafting, so Brody's chances were about the same as Callum's—fifty-fifty. But Teague knew Hayley would throw herself headlong into any competition, especially if it involved riding.

"Two on a horse," Brody explained. "The girls steer, the guys work the stirrups. This should be fun."

Teague reached down and grabbed Hayley's arm, then swung her up in front of him. "We've got this won," he whispered in her ear.

"I don't know," Hayley said. "I think Payton might be a decent rider."

"And you could probably beat half the stockmen," he said. "With your hands tied behind your back."

"Oh, adding a little bondage to the competition might be fun," Hayley teased.

"Be careful," he warned, holding her close. "I won't be able to concentrate on winning."

Callum decided to go first and called out to Davey to release a calf from the pen. Payton and Brody watched from the other side of the fence, Brody's arms wrapped around Payton's waist and his chin resting on her shoulder.

Gemma screamed as she tried to maneuver Callum's horse. When Callum tried to grab the reins, the stockmen began to jeer at him for cheating. He finally told Gemma to drop the reins and he steered his horse using only his knees and feet.

Though the effort wasn't Callum's best, he did manage to get the calf through the obstacle course and back into the pen in under five minutes. Gemma looked as if she could hardly wait to get off the horse.

"Hey!" Brody called from the fence. "We're going to grab some more coldies. Who wants one?"

Both Hayley and Teague raised their hands, as did half the stockmen. Brody took Payton's hand and pulled her along toward the house.

"I sure hope you boys aren't too thirsty," Callum shouted. "They may be a while."

Teague gave Tapper a gentle kick and Hayley maneuvered the horse over to the gate. "Ready?" Teague asked.

"I'm ready."

Teague shouted to Davey and a moment later, the gate swung open and a calf ran out. Teague jabbed his heels into Tapper's sides and Hayley pulled the horse to the right, cutting off the calf's escape.

Over the next ninety seconds, they worked as a perfect team, anticipating each other's movements without speaking. Hayley was firm but aggressive with the reins, and Teague couldn't help but admire her determination. When they returned the calf to the pen and Davey slammed the gate shut, the stockmen erupted in wild cheers.

Teague glanced over at Callum to find his brother looking at the two of them in disbelief. "What?" Teague said. "You didn't think we could do it?"

"You beat Skip's time and he's the best on Kerry Creek," Callum said. "Ninety seconds."

"No," Teague replied, shaking his head. "You must have the time wrong. Skip Thompson's the best stockman we have. No one can beat him." He reached around Hayley and took the reins, then trotted Tapper over to the gate.

"It was only ninety seconds," Hayley said beneath her breath. "I think we won."

"I know. But we can't humiliate the boys. Skip will get the prize and everyone will be happy."

"What about my prize?" she said, turning around and sending him a sexy pout.

"I'll think of something I can do to make it up to you."

"You could rub my backside," Hayley suggested. "I've been spending too much time riding and I'm a bit sore."

When they reached the stable, Teague helped Hayley off his horse, then removed Tapper's saddle. He led him into the stable yard, then carried the saddle to the tack room. When he emerged, Hayley was waiting for him, a devilish smile on her pretty face.

"I'm not going to rub your bum," he said.

"Please," Hayley teased. She turned away from him, then looked over her shoulder, pursing her lips in another pretty pout.

Hayley was growing less wary of him, he mused. Allowing herself to tease and act playful. Maybe they were making progress. Teague was still unsure, but as long as their relationship kept changing for the better, he wasn't going to complain. "What if someone walks in?" he asked.

She pulled him into an empty stall. Then, taking his wrists, she placed both of his palms on her backside. Wriggling, she pressed up against him, her arms draped around his neck. "You do it so well when I'm naked. What's a little denim between friends?"

"Friends with benefits," he reminded her. "You really are determined to make me squirm, aren't you? Is this payback for my dragging you here in the first place?"

"No. Actually, I'm having a lovely time. Gemma and Payton are very nice and your brothers have been quite cordial."

"I told you you'd have fun."

"I'd have more fun if you rubbed my bum."

With a low growl, Teague grabbed her legs and picked her up, wrapping her thighs around his waist. Hayley yelped with surprise, then laughed as he stumbled. Pressing her against the wooden wall, Teague kissed her, his hands smoothing over the sweet curves of her backside.

"Oh, yes," Hayley moaned, her voice deep and dramatic. "Oh, that feels so good."

"I thought you were a good actress," Teague teased.

She pushed her hands against his shoulders and looked at him, a shocked expression on her pretty features. "And I thought you were a good lover."

"I am," Teague said.

"Prove it."

It was like one of those challenges she used to issue when they were kids—I can ride faster than you can, I can jump higher than you can, I can hold my breath longer than you can. He'd never refused one of her challenges in the past and he wasn't about to now.

"Here?"

"Are you afraid? Oh, don't be such a big girl's blouse."

"And you're going to get a reputation as the town bike if you don't watch out." He chuckled as he set her back on her feet. "I'm not going to start something here that might be interrupted, especially by one of my brothers."

"Then you'll have to work quickly," she said, reaching down and unbuttoning his jeans. "Ingenious design, these chaps. Good for riding and better for sex."

He moaned softly as she began to tease him erect. Strange how the prospect of getting caught made the desire even more intense. It was silly, this desperate need to hide their sexual relationship. Their romance was in the open now and there didn't seem to be any objections from the Quinn side of the equation. And sex was all part of that.

Still, Teague wasn't anxious for his brothers to know how obsessed he was with Hayley Fraser. She'd become the single point around which his universe revolved. And he was beginning to believe that he wouldn't want to live his life any other way.

"So what are you looking for in the way of a massage?" Teague whispered, his lips trailing along the curve of her neck.

She drew in a slow breath, then tipped her head to the side, inviting him to move lower. "I'll leave that up to you."

Over the next minute, they tore at each other's clothes, pulling aside just enough to allow the basics of sex. And when he slipped inside her, Teague was already on the edge. This was all he needed in life. That thought whirled round and round in his head as her warmth enveloped him.

And when he finally lost control and buried himself one last time, he made a silent promise. He would do whatever it took to make her happy, whatever it took to keep her with him. She was his—she always had been, from the moment they'd met out on the big rock until forever.

HAYLEY HEARD THE PLANE before she saw it. Shading her eyes from the sun, she stared up into the sky and caught sight of it coming in from the west. He flew low over the house and she ran out into the yard and waved. Teague wiggled the wings in response.

With a laugh, she hurried to her car and hopped inside, then made a wide turn toward the old airstrip. It had been a week since the queen's birthday celebration and she and Teague had seen each other only a few times. His work had called him off the station several times on overnight visits, and when he returned, he was off again within the next few hours. On top of that, he'd had to make a quick flight with Payton and Brody to Brisbane when they'd decided to visit Fremantle for a few days.

Though Hayley knew this was what a real relationship between them would be like, she'd found herself feeling more lonely than she'd ever imagined she could. No matter how hard she tried to convince herself they were involved in a purely physical relationship, it was becoming more delusion now than determination.

She and Teague weren't just sexual partners. They'd rediscovered their friendship and rekindled an affection that had never really disappeared. And though it might have been easy to say they were falling in love again, Hayley wasn't ready to take that step—not yet. Perhaps if they could meet the challenge of spending so much time apart, she might consider love.

The odds had been against them when they were kids and now that they were adults, not much had changed. She had her career in Sydney and the possibility of much more. And he had his new practice in Bilbarra. Perhaps if Teague had been free to practice in Sydney, it might work between them.

But he'd made a commitment to buy Doc Daley's practice. It was his chance to run his own business. And it could take years to establish himself in Sydney, especially as an equine vet. He'd probably be forced to join an existing practice and work for someone else. This had been his dream, to live in Queensland, to expand the horse-breeding operation on Kerry Creek.

He was standing beside the plane when she arrived at the airstrip, his arm braced on one of the wing struts. Hayley hopped out of the car and walked up to him. "Are you trying to impress me?" she asked in a teasing voice.

"Come on," he said. "Let's go."

"Where are we going?"

"We're getting away. You and me, alone, for a few days. I've made all the regular visits on my schedule and now I've got some time."

"I can't just leave," she said. "I don't have anything packed and I—"

"You won't need anything," Teague said.

"But—"

"But what? Where's your sense of adventure, Hayley Fraser? As I recall, you called me a big girl's blouse just last week. You used to do anything on a dare. I dare you to get in this plane."

"I can't leave without telling Harry I'm going to be gone. He'll notice I'm not there to make him supper."

"All right. Go," Teague said. "I'll give you fifteen minutes. If you're not back, I'm going to leave without you. I'll have to find another girl who's more adventurous."

Hayley frowned. Then she stepped up to him, threw her arms around his neck and kissed him. The kiss was long and deep and meant to show him that leaving her behind would be a big mistake. When she finally drew away, she looked up into his eyes to see desire burning there.

"Yeah, I thought so. You're not going to leave," she assured him. "And there are no other girls more adventurous than I am."

A smile curled the corners of his mouth and he sighed. "No. But I still want you to hurry."

"Are you going to tell me where we're going?"

He grinned and shook his head. "Do you have something against surprises?"

Hayley usually preferred to be in control, but she knew Teague would never plan a surprise she wouldn't like. "I'll be right back."

By the time Hayley returned to the house, Harry was already pacing a path along the length of the porch. When he saw the car, he stopped and stormed into the yard. "Where did you go?" he demanded as she jumped out of the car. "Was that a plane I heard?"

"Yes. I'm going to be leaving for a few days. I have…business. It's important, so they sent a plane." It was an outright lie, but Hayley didn't want to take the time to make up a more plausible excuse. She paused. Maybe she ought to tell Harry the truth. There was no use hiding it anymore. "That's not right," she said, facing him. "Teague Quinn has invited me on a holiday and I'm going. I don't care if you don't like it. I'm an adult and I make my own decisions."

Harry cursed and wagged his finger. "I'll not have you taking up with that Quinn boy again!" he shouted.

"I can do what I want, Harry. There'll be no letters for you to intercept and no phone calls for you to ignore. I've cooked and cleaned for you for the past two weeks and I deserve a bit of a break. I'll be home… when I get home."

She moved to the door, ready to return to her room and pack a few belongings. But then, Hayley realized she'd only have to put up with Harry's badgering the whole time. Teague said she wouldn't need anything, so she would trust him on that, as well.

"Goodbye, Harry." Hayley jogged down the steps and got into her car. She saw Harry in the rearview mirror, glaring at her from his spot on the porch. She'd never really stood up to him when it came to Teague and now that she had, Hayley realized Harry wasn't nearly as powerful as she'd thought he was. What was the worst he could do, kick her out of the house? She had a place of her own in Sydney. And a place with Teague, if she needed it.

Harry would have the next few days to cool off before she had to face him again. But there was no longer a reason for her to be ashamed of seeing Teague. He made her happy and she hadn't felt truly happy since the last time they'd been together. Nearly ten years of searching for the one thing she needed, and she found it in the place where it had all begun.

When she drove up to the plane, Teague was waiting. He helped her inside, showing her how to strap in, then circled around and climbed into the pilot's seat. A few seconds later, the engine roared to life.

"When did you learn how to fly?" she shouted.

"Four years ago," he said. "Figured I'd need a plane if I was going to be an outback vet. I bought it last year.

Lived like a pauper when I was working in Brisbane, saving everything I made. This baby comes in handy."

Hayley had never been in a small plane before. She drew a deep breath as they headed down the bumpy runway, the plane gathering speed. She was afraid it might fall apart with all the bouncing and bumping, but then they lifted off and the ride was suddenly smooth.

Teague reached over and captured her hand, then brought it to his lips to kiss it. She felt a familiar thrill, the same feeling she'd had when they were kids and they'd found an adventure to experience together. There was a certain satisfaction in sharing something new with Teague. As if it was something no one could ever take from them.

"Will you tell me where we're going now?"

He shook his head. "Look in the bags behind your seat."

She twisted around and found two huge shopping bags from David Jones, a department-store chain. "What's this?"

"I picked up a few things while I was shopping with the girls."

"How long have you been planning this?"

He shrugged. "Awhile. Well, ever since we spent that first night in the shack. I wasn't sure I'd be able to get away, but Doc Daley told me I could take a few days if I cleared my schedule."

She pulled out a tiny pink-flowered bikini and held it up. "We're going to the beach?"

"Yes." He nodded.

She found a matching sarong and a pretty pair of sandals in the same bag. In the other bag, she found two sundresses along with a pale yellow cotton cardie. In a smaller bag, a selection of underwear, bras and panties in pastel colors. "You bought these yourself?"

He nodded again. "I think they'll fit. I had to guess on the sizes." He glanced over at her. "I don't think you'll need more than that."

"I suspect I'll be spending a fair number of hours without any clothes at all."

"Yes," he agreed with a boyish grin. "I didn't pack much, either."

As they flew northeast, Teague pointed out all the major landmarks. They flew over Carnarvon National Park and then over the Blackdown Tablelands before turning directly north. Soon, the coast was visible, the turquoise-blue water shimmering in the afternoon sun. Hayley sat back in her seat, watching the landscape float by below them. When they got over the water, Teague brought the plane lower and pointed out the window at a pod of whales breaking the smooth surface. They circled once so she could get a better look, then he navigated north again.

"It's so beautiful," she said. "I love the ocean."

"I know." He turned and smiled at her. "You told me the day we met. You stood on the top of the rock and tried to see the ocean. And when you couldn't, I was afraid you might cry."

"You remember that?"

"I remember everything about that day," he said.

Islands dotted the coastline and Teague headed farther east until they could see waves breaking over the Great Barrier Reef. She'd never really appreciated the true beauty of her homeland, but here, with Teague, everything looked different somehow. The coast was greener, the sky bluer, the water sparkling with the light of a million diamonds.

How was it possible that life seemed so much more exciting when he was near? He was just a man, nothing more. Yet, when she was with him, she felt…complete. As if all the pieces that had been missing over the years had found their place again in her heart.

Her body buzzed with a strange anticipation. While they were on Wallaroo and Kerry Creek, it was simple to think of their time together in finite terms. But now that they were in the real world, the possibilities seemed endless. Could they continue after they both returned to their regular lives? Would there be shared holidays and weekends away? The more she thought about how it might work, the more Hayley realized that it could work.

Lots of people carried on long-distance relationships. And she and Teague had spent nearly ten years apart, yet it hadn't changed anything between them, except the intensity of their feelings for each other. What was a week or a month compared to ten years?

"Which beach are we going to?" she asked.

"Why don't you let me surprise you," he insisted. "I know it's not in your nature, but give it a try, just this once."

"I have to warn you again that wherever we go,

people will recognize me. They'll either ask for my autograph or tell me what a horrible person I am. They sometimes get me mixed up with my character."

"You *are* a very bad girl on the program. How many marriages have you destroyed?"

"Three, I think," Hayley said ruefully. "And two engagements. I seem to like sex far too much for my own good."

"How does that work?" Teague asked. "When you have to do those scenes?"

"Sometimes it's uncomfortable. Especially when you don't know the other person very well. But it's part of the job." She paused. "And sometimes, it creates a false sense of intimacy."

"And how did the men in your life handle you doing love scenes with other guys?"

"You mean my boyfriends?"

Teague nodded. "I know you've had boyfriends. I've read all the magazines. Whenever there was a story about you and some fella, I'd have to read it. You've had some very famous boyfriends."

"I suppose they didn't care. They never really knew me, anyway. I never let them get close enough."

"I know what you mean," Teague said. "It's never felt right with other women."

"So you were abstinent for ten years," she joked.

"No. And I don't expect you were, either. But I never found anyone that felt as…right as you did. As right as you *do*. With me."

"What are we going to do about that?" she asked.

"I don't know. I'm still figuring it out."

A long silence grew between them as Hayley considered what he'd told her. Everything he'd said had been the truth and she'd felt it as strongly as he had. They belonged together. But admitting that fact made everything so much more complicated.

She could figure it all out later, she decided. For the next few days, she was going to enjoy her time with Teague and not worry about the future.

6

TEAGUE SAT on the edge of the bed and stared out the open doors onto the bungalow's wide veranda. Hayley stood facing the ocean, her body outlined by the setting sun. The breeze caught a strand of her hair and he watched as she distractedly tucked it behind her ear.

She was the most beautiful thing he'd ever seen. And it was obvious to him that he couldn't consider a life without her. How was that possible? Had they really fallen in love as teenagers? Was this merely a continuation of those feelings? If he couldn't figure that out here, alone with her, then maybe he'd never know for sure.

They'd landed at the only commercial airport in the Whitsundays, on Hamilton Island, and then had hopped onto a helicopter for the ten-minute flight to the resort. Teague had heard of the resort when he was living in Brisbane and when he'd called to make a reservation, he'd been assured that it was very private. There were only sixteen bungalows, set near the water's edge, the lush rain forest spreading out behind them. This being the off-season, he and Hayley were the only guests midweek.

The bungalows were furnished in plantation style with high ceilings and polished wood floors. A fan whirred above his head, the sound mixing with the rush of waves on the shore. If they were going to fall in love all over again, this would be the place to do it, Teague mused. They had three days and nights together to figure out their relationship.

She turned to face him, her expression soft and her smile satisfied. "It's beautiful," Hayley said as she walked toward him.

"The helicopter pilot told me we're the only guests right now. We have the whole island to ourselves. Besides the staff, the wallabies, the goannas and—"

She put her finger to his lips, then sat down on his lap. "No people to bother me with autographs," she said.

"Nope."

"A real bed with a down comforter," she said, leaning back to smooth her hand over the bed linens.

Teague nodded.

"You know how to spoil a girl, don't you."

"I do my best," he said.

She gave his chest a gentle shove and they tumbled onto the bed together. "Now that we're here, what are we going to do with ourselves?"

"I have some ideas," Teague teased. "But they all involve taking off your clothes."

Hayley scrambled to her feet and, without hesitation, pulled the cotton dress up and over her head. Then she kicked off her shoes and jumped onto the bed. "Now what?"

"Use your imagination," Teague said.

She stretched out at his side, then ran her hand from his chest to his groin. She rubbed the front of his khakis, waiting for the customary reaction to her touch. As he grew hard, she smiled. "You're far too easy," she said.

Teague caught her wrists and rolled her beneath him, pinning her hands above her head. "What about you? It doesn't take much to make you all warm and wet."

"I can last longer than you can," she said.

Another challenge. Funny how he enjoyed these challenges so much more than the silly challenges of their younger years. He loosened his grip on her wrists and slowly slid down along her body, his lips pressing against her silken skin. He stopped long enough to dispense with her bra, then let his mouth linger over each tempting breast.

Hayley arched beneath him as he brought each nipple to a stiff peak, then blew on it softly. Teague's fingers twisted in the waistband of her panties as he pulled them over her hips and thighs. When she was finally naked, he lay beside her and gently caressed the damp spot between her legs.

Her eyes were closed and her lips slightly parted. When he looked at her, every detail of her face suddenly became important to him. Her bow-shaped upper lip, the long lashes that fluttered against her cheeks, the tiny mole on her chin. He'd known them all by heart so many years ago, but now he didn't want to forget.

Teague bent over and kissed her gently as he slipped

his finger inside her. Hayley's breath caught in her throat and she moaned. He knew she was close, but he wanted to prolong her pleasure. They had a comfortable bed and a long night ahead of them. There was no need to rush.

But Hayley wasn't ready to surrender. She gently pushed his hand away, then rolled over and straddled his body. Her hair fell in waves around her face and she smiled down at him as she tugged at his T-shirt.

Carefully, she undressed him, Teague touching her at every turn, his hands searching out the sweet curves of her body. He'd been so long without a woman before Hayley had come into his life again. And now that he'd grown used to having her near, Teague wondered if he'd ever be able to do without. There was something so comforting in knowing that, for at least this moment in time, she belonged entirely to him.

Her lips were warm against his bare skin. A shiver skittered over him as she teased his nipple. Then, her lips drifted lower until her hair tickled his belly. He knew her game but he also knew how close he was to losing control. Teague groaned as her mouth brushed along the length of his shaft.

There were certain aspects of passion that they hadn't enjoyed as teenagers and this had been one of them. But it was obvious that new skills had been acquired in ten years. Her mouth closed around him and Teague felt a current race through his body, making him flinch in response.

He slid his fingers through her hair, holding her back when he felt too close, then loosening his grip when he wanted more. Teague lost himself in the wild sensations her mouth and hands were bringing him.

"All right," he groaned. "You win."

"Not yet," Hayley said. "Not until you give up." She went to work and Teague knew she wouldn't be satisfied until he was. Did he want to surrender? Or would he rather find his release inside her?

In the end, Teague didn't have a choice. The feel of her tongue on his cock was more than he could handle. He held his breath and felt his body grow tense with anticipation. And then, a spasm shook his core. His fingers tangled in her hair, gently pulling her away as the warmth of his orgasm pooled on his belly.

When it was finally over and his body had relaxed, Teague opened his eyes to find her looking up at him, her chin resting on his chest. "I win," she said, a satisfied smile on her face.

"No. I'm pretty sure I won that round." He reached down and drew her up alongside him, tucking her into the curve of his arm. "If this is any indication of the rest of our holiday, I think I'm going to need a holiday from our holiday."

"I like this," she said, staring up at the ceiling. "It feels so grown-up."

"We are grown-up," Teague said.

"Sometimes I don't feel like an adult. I keep waiting for my life to start, as if there's supposed to be a big sign that tells me when I need to begin paying attention. Your Life Starts Now," she said, emphasizing each word with her hands.

"Your life has started."

"But it doesn't seem like it's mine," Hayley said. "It feels like it belongs to someone else."

"What did you think it was supposed to be?"

She considered his question for a long moment. "I thought that you and I would live on a station and we'd raise horses and spend all day riding them. And at night, we'd live in a little shack, like the one on Wallaroo. And we'd sleep in the same bed and wake up together every morning. And that would be our life."

"It sounds pretty nice to me," Teague said.

"Not very practical, though. Where would we have found the money to buy a station and horses? How would we have supported ourselves? It was a silly dream."

Not so silly, Teague thought to himself. He'd had the same dream himself when he was younger. Only, he'd have a job as a vet to help support them both. They'd work the station together and breed the best horses in all of Australia.

But as he looked at Hayley now, he wondered whether she'd be happy with station life. He'd seen what it had done to his own mother, driving her away after eighteen years of marriage. And raising a family in the outback wasn't a piece of cake, either.

Hayley had a glamorous life in Sydney, enough money to live quite comfortably. She was a celebrity, people recognized her. That wasn't the kind of life someone walked away from.

But he could walk away and join her. His deal with Doc Daley wasn't finalized yet. Though they'd reached a verbal agreement, they were due to sign the papers at the end of the month. If he backed out, there would certainly be other vets who'd jump at the chance to take over the practice. Teague could return to clinic work, like he'd done after he graduated from vet school. City life hadn't been that bad. He could get used to caring for dogs and cats again and forget about horses.

Teague closed his eyes. He'd promised himself that he wouldn't think about the future while they were at the resort. There was time enough for that later.

"There's a very large shower in the bathroom. I think we should try it out," he said.

"We've never had a shower together," she said. "Or a bath."

"Well, if you don't count the time you snuck over to the pond on Kerry Creek and talked me into skinny-dipping."

A smile spread slowly across her pretty face. "I remember that."

"Yes. You spent half the night laughing at the effect the cold water had on my bits and pieces. I was humiliated."

"Yes, but you forget that a few days later, we found something much more interesting to do with your bits and pieces." She dropped a kiss on his lips. "We had sex for the first time."

"That's right," he said. "And look where we are now. Still naked, still having sex. And you're still issuing challenges."

"We have come a long way," Hayley said. She rolled off the bed and held out her hand. "Shower. I think it's time we ticked that off the list. I'll wager you dinner that I can wash your back better than you can wash mine."

Teague followed her into the bathroom, his gaze fixed on the sweet curve of her backside. If this was the way their holiday was starting, three days and nights would never be enough.

HAYLEY SAT on the wooden lounge chair, her feet tucked under her. The sun was beginning to brighten the morning sky. The mist rising from the dense rain forest on the island would soon burn off, leaving them with another beautiful day.

She'd learned to love mornings on the island. Right before the sun came up, birds would awaken and begin chattering in the trees that surrounded their bungalow. Teague slept so deeply he never noticed. But for Hayley, they were like an alarm clock, reminding her that she had another whole day to spend with Teague.

They'd walk on the beach or take a trek on the paths through the forest. They'd sip fresh juice for breakfast and enjoy a gourmet meal for dinner.

Sadly, this was their last day on the island. At noon, they'd take the helicopter back to Hamilton Island and then Teague's plane home to Wallaroo. She didn't want their holiday to end. It had all been too perfect.

Was she wrong to believe that real life would never match the fantasy of their time on the island? It was easy to fall in love in this place. They had no responsibilities, no worries, no careers tugging them in different directions.

Was their relationship strong enough to survive time

and distance apart? If they didn't make any promises to each other, there wouldn't be any failures or regrets. Why couldn't she accept this for what it was—temporary?

If she knew what was good for her, she'd return to Sydney before she lost her heart completely. She had scripts to memorize and she hadn't been to the gym in ages. Plus, she'd promised her agent she'd make the trip to L.A. before she was due back on the set.

She pushed to her feet and walked inside the room, the dew from the veranda creating tracks across the wooden floor. Slipping out of the expensive robe that the resort provided, she crawled beneath the down comforter.

Teague was warm, his naked body stretched out beneath the cotton sheets. This was the third morning she'd awoken beside him without having to think about the repercussions of spending the night together. This was how it should be.

Hayley slid her arm around his waist and pressed her body against his, throwing her leg over his thigh. He stirred and then slowly opened his eyes, turning his sleepy gaze on her.

"Your feet are freezing," he complained.

"I was sitting out on the veranda. Listening to the birds."

"What time is it?"

"Early, she said. "The sun is just coming up."

"I like waking up with you," Teague said, drawing her closer.

"How would it have been," Hayley asked, "if I had come to Perth to be with you?"

Teague frowned. "What brought this on?"

"I'm curious. How would it have worked?"

He drew a deep breath then raked his hand through his tousled hair. "Well. We would have had to find a place to live. I don't think they would have allowed you to stay in my room at Murdoch. We would have found a flat in the city, something we could afford. I worked while I was in school, so we would have had some money, although my parents might have cut me off if they'd known we were together. You would have had to find a job. I'm not sure we could have both afforded to go to school, but I could have—"

Hayley reached up and pressed her finger to his lips, stopping his words. "Do you realize how complicated it would have been? Teague, it would never have worked. As much as we dreamed it could."

"You don't know that," he said.

"I found a job when I first got to Sydney and I could barely afford to eat, never mind rent a place to live. We were so young and so stupid. We thought love would solve all our problems. Love doesn't pay the bills. It was best that things turned out the way they did, don't you think?"

"We spent ten years apart," Teague reminded her.

"But we both made something of ourselves in that time. We're happy with our lives, aren't we?" she asked.

"Are you? You don't seem anxious to get back to yours."

"Don't try to analyze me," she warned. "Best leave that to professionals."

He sighed softly. "I wish I could find a bandage to

fix all the bad things that happened to you in your life, Hayley. I wish there was medicine or some kind of cure for all the pain that you've had to endure."

"I know I'm pretty much a wreck," she said with a weak smile. "It's a wonder you can tolerate me. But don't stop trying."

"You're not a wreck. You're a little banged up. A few dents here and there, but nothing that will stop me from wanting you."

"So do you think you can fix me, Dr. Feelgood?"

"I'm Dr. Feelamazinglygood." He pulled his hand out from under the comforter. "These fingers are magic. They can cure anything that ails you."

"What about what ails you?" Hayley slipped her hand beneath the comforter and smoothed it along his belly until she found his shaft, which was already growing hard with desire. "I think you have a problem. Something very strange is happening here. There's an unusual swelling. Oh dear, I've never seen anything like it."

"Very strange," he said, kissing her softly.

Hayley giggled, then felt a warm blush creep up her cheeks. "I remember the first time I touched you down there. I had absolutely no idea. I mean, I'd seen horses and cattle, but I never imagined that boys would function the same way."

"Are you saying I resemble a stallion? Or a bull?"

"Oh, definitely a stallion," she said. "Long legs, a nice mane, beautiful eyes."

"So, you want to go for a ride or what?"

Hayley gasped at his request, then gave him a playful slap. "You're terrible. All you think about is sex."

"No, all I think about is sex with you. There's a big difference."

"You don't ever think about other women?"

"Not since you came back into my life. You're it. All my fantasies, you're right there. Dressed in sexy lingerie, doing all kinds of nasty things to me, whispering in my ear, telling me how much you want me."

"We need to take another holiday together," she said. "This has been perfect."

"It would be this way all the time if we lived together," he said.

Hayley shook her head. "You'd toss me out in less than a week. I'd make a horrible roommate." She knew what he was offering, but if she made a joke of it, she wouldn't have to answer him.

She sighed inwardly. She'd like nothing more than to accept. It would be wonderful to share a place and to share their lives. But marriage was difficult enough, even without long periods apart. If she was going to commit to Teague, then she'd have to be prepared to give up her life in Sydney and start a new life with him.

"You haven't been a bad roommate these last few days. I wish we could stay longer," he said.

"Me, too. I'm not looking forward to my homecoming at Wallaroo. In fact, I've been thinking maybe you ought to fly me straight to Sydney."

"You want to go home to Sydney?" he asked, a trace of hurt in his voice.

"No. It's just that…I told Harry about us. Right before I left. That I was going away with you. I'm not sure if he's going to want me staying with him anymore."

"Why did you do that?"

"I was tired of pretending. It was silly. And you and I have nothing to do with the fight between him and Callum. So what difference does it make?"

"He won't see it that way," Teague said.

Hayley shrugged. "I expect all my things will be tossed in a big pile in the yard. Or maybe he'll have burned them. When he's given enough time, he can work up a pretty bad temper."

"The longer that feud goes on, the more ridiculous it seems."

"It's a matter of honor," Hayley said.

"What are you talking about?"

She pressed her face into his naked chest. "That's what Harry says. It's a matter of honor. Promises were made and promises were broken."

"What promises?"

"You don't know?"

"No. I assumed it was some mistake made on the deed years ago."

"According to Harry, his father traded a mail-order bride for that piece of land. Your great-grandmother fell in love with your great-grandfather and didn't want to marry my great-grandfather. So they made a trade. Only, your great-grandfather kept the land and the girl."

"Why did I never know that story?"

"Probably because it proves that Harry is right about

the land. It belongs to Wallaroo. Unfortunately, the paperwork was never filed. It was a gentleman's agreement, which doesn't count for much these days." She glanced over at him. "So, I guess that if it weren't for my great-grandfather and that little piece of land, you and your brothers wouldn't exist."

Teague frowned. "I'm not sure I believe anything Harry says. He'd do anything to have his way."

"It is a good story, though. Especially if it proves to be true."

"Maybe I should trade Harry the land for you," Teague teased, nuzzling her neck. "That would end the feud and we'd both get what we wanted."

"What about what I want?" Hayley said. "Doesn't that count?"

Teague pulled back, his gaze searching her face. "What do you want, Hayley?"

It was a simple question and Hayley ought to give him an answer. She could tell he was getting weary of always asking where he stood. And truly, if she knew, she'd give him an answer. But fabulous sex and long, romantic meals with Teague had only made her more confused. It wasn't just about a relationship now, it was about a lifetime together.

"Breakfast might be nice," she said.

"Don't do that," Teague warned. "Don't brush me off like that. Whenever I talk about the future, you seem to find a way to make a joke out of it. We've spent three incredible days together, just the two of us and no one else. Has that made any difference?"

She tried to twist out of his arms, but Teague wouldn't let her go. "Hayley, I'm falling in love with you all over again. But you've got to let me know if I'm making a fool of myself. Or if there's a chance for us."

"Don't do this," she said. "I can't— I don't know how—"

"What?"

"I can't go through that all again. Watching you walk out of my life. I can't do it."

"But you won't have to. That's the point. If we decide to be together, then that's it. Neither one of us will be walking out."

"I will be. All the time. My work doesn't exactly allow me to stay in one place for very long. Not if I want to be successful."

"Is acting what you want to do for the rest of your life?"

"I'm not sure. But my career is the only thing in this world that truly belongs to me. I made it happen. And I don't think I can give that up."

He exhaled slowly and drew her closer. "All right. At least I know where we stand on that. And I'm all right with a long-distance thing. You'll come home when you can. We can make it work, Hayley."

"Are you going to come to Sydney? Are you going to follow me around the world when I have work outside Australia? Would you give up everything to be with me?"

"I'm not sure I'd have to give up everything," Teague said. "We don't need to be together every minute of every day in order to be happy."

Hayley felt tears of frustration pushing at the corners

of her eyes. "Oh, brilliant," she muttered. "Now I'm crying again. I seem to do that a lot lately."

Teague ran his hands through her hair, then dropped a soft kiss on her lips. "Don't cry. There's no need for tears."

"I just…can't."

"I know," he murmured, pressing a kiss to her temple and then another to each of her eyelids. "I know."

Hayley drew in a ragged breath, then let the tears come. She had fought so long against her emotions. But now that they'd finally broken free, she realized how much good came of crying. It felt as if all the pain was draining out in her tears.

Teague held her close as she wept. After a time, she wasn't sure why she was still crying. Was it for her parents? For the perfect childhood she'd never had? For the love and loyalty that Teague was so determined to give her?

It didn't matter. All that mattered was that she was finally capable of crying. And whether Teague understood her tears or not, the ability to let loose her emotions meant more to their future than anything she might say.

"I CAN'T BELIEVE we have to leave in a few hours," Hayley said. She glanced up at Teague and then reached across the breakfast table to take his hand. "This was the best holiday I've ever had. Thank you."

"Next time it will be your turn to plan," he said. "I'll provide the plane."

"All right," Hayley agreed. "It's a date. No matter what happens, we'll have another holiday together."

"And then another and another," Teague said. "We

could survive on a string of holidays." He paused. "I would be satisfied with that if that's what you're offering."

Teague felt like a fool willing to settle for scraps when he might have the entire meal. But if it was what Hayley wanted, he didn't have much choice.

She nodded. "We'll choose a date and I'll make the plans. And this time, it will be my treat."

"Christmas," he said. "I'd like to spend Christmas with you."

"Christmas it is."

They finished their breakfast in silence. Teague was happy they'd managed to agree on future plans at last. But it hadn't escaped him that the plans didn't address the things standing between them and a real relationship.

In a few weeks, he would sign the papers that would give him ownership of Doc Daley's practice. When he'd first returned to Kerry Creek, Teague had been certain that taking over an established practice would be the perfect opportunity. Doc Daley had been ready to retire, and Teague figured he could make enough to buy Doc out in five years. He already had the plane, so he could handle much more business than Doc had ever managed, which would increase his income substantially. His future had looked brilliant.

But now Teague had to wonder if tying himself down in Queensland was really the answer. He could establish a practice on the outskirts of any large city—Brisbane, Sydney, Melbourne. Or he could work for another vet and not worry about keeping a business afloat.

Funny how he'd spent the last ten years of his life

happily cruising along, never worrying about his future. It was easy when he was on his own, with no responsibilities for another person. But he'd begun to see how complicated things could become once he'd decided on a life with Hayley.

Hell, there was no point thinking about it now. He had a few weeks. Things might be completely different between them by then. They'd just planned a holiday together. Who knew what could be waiting around the next corner?

"Mr. Quinn?"

Teague looked up at the waiter. "We're fine. The breakfast was great." He glanced over at Hayley. "Would you like more juice?"

She shook her head. "No. Thank you."

"Mr. Quinn, there's a phone call for you in the office. It's a Dr. Daley. He says it's urgent."

Teague frowned. He'd nearly forgotten they'd been without phones for the past three days. Messages were delivered in person. No telephones, no television, nothing to distract from the solitude.

He pushed away from the table. "This will only take a minute," he said to Hayley. "He's probably wondering if I can make a call on my way home to the station."

He followed the waiter to the small office where the manager was waiting with the phone. "Thanks," Teague said. "Doc?"

"Sorry to interrupt your holiday, Teague."

"No worries. Is something wrong?"

"I got a call from Cal early this morning. He's been

looking for you and thought I might know where you were."

He'd told his brother that he'd be gone until Friday afternoon. He hadn't given him all the details, but had assumed he wouldn't be bothered with station business. "I'll call him. I'm sorry that he—"

"No, he wanted me to pass along a message. This is for Hayley Fraser. She is with you, isn't she?"

"Yes," Teague said.

"Hayley's grandfather took a bad fall. He rode over to Kerry Creek and wanted to stir things up with Cal. He fell getting off his horse and broke his hip. He's in the hospital in Brisbane. Things aren't looking too good. He's refusing care and insisting that they let him go home. They want Hayley there as soon as possible to try to talk some sense into him."

"Which hospital?" Teague asked.

"St. Andrew's."

"Call Cal and tell him we'll get there as soon as we can."

"Take a few more days to be with your girl," Doc said. "I can handle things here."

"Thanks," Teague said. He returned the cordless phone to the manager. "Can we get an earlier flight to Hamilton? We've got a bit of an emergency."

"I'll call the pilot right now," the manager said. "Why don't you get packed and I'll send someone to let you know when the helicopter will arrive."

Teague hurried back to the dining room. This was going to be difficult. Hayley had finally asserted herself with her grandfather and now she'd get drawn in again by guilt. Teague wasn't sure how she'd react to the news.

She saw his expression before he had a chance to sit down. "What's wrong?"

He took a deep breath. "It's your grandfather. He must have rode Molly over to Kerry Creek. He was looking to mix it up with Cal, probably over the land dispute. He somehow fell off Molly and broke his hip."

Hayley gasped. "Oh, no. That's serious, isn't it?"

Teague nodded. "They've taken him to the hospital in Brisbane. But he's refusing treatment. They want you to come and convince him."

"He has a broken hip. He can't walk with a broken hip. What does he expect to do?"

"I don't know, Hayley. But we need to go there. The resort manager is calling for the helicopter. We can fly directly to Brisbane from Hamilton. We'll be there in a few hours."

"Could he die from a broken hip?" Hayley asked.

"No," Teague said. It was the truth. But Teague knew the complications that came with an injury like that. For a man Harry's age there was pneumonia and blood clots to consider. And if he refused treatment, he'd be stuck in a wheelchair for the rest of his life, probably living in a great deal of pain.

Teague stood and held out his hand and Hayley laced her fingers through his. "Everything will be all right," he said.

Hayley nodded, her face pale and her eyes wide. He walked to the room with her, then packed for both of them while Hayley stood on the veranda, looking out at the ocean. Without her grandfather on Wallaroo, there was little to keep her in Queensland.

Teague said a silent prayer that the old man would see reason and accept treatment for his injury. Maybe, with rehab, he could live on his own. But it was unlikely he'd be fit to run Wallaroo again. Chances were far better that Hayley would have to find him a place where she could watch over him.

A soft knock sounded at the door and Teague pulled it open. The resort manager stood there, a solemn expression on his face. "The helicopter will be here in ten minutes. Would you like me to take your bags?"

Teague nodded, then stepped aside to let him pass. The manager gathered up their meager belongings. "I'm sorry your holiday had to end so abruptly," he said.

"I am, too," Teague said. "But it's been wonderful. Truly, the best holiday I've ever had."

"We hope you'll come again soon."

Teague closed the door behind the manager and walked across the room to the veranda door. "Ten minutes," he said.

Hayley turned around. Her face was wet with tears. In three long strides, he crossed the veranda and gathered her into his arms. "Don't worry," he whispered. "Everything will be fine."

"Promise?"

"I promise. Harry is being stubborn. It always takes him a while before he gives in."

"He's not going to want to see me. He thinks I deserted him. For you."

"Well, now you're coming back. And if he doesn't forgive you, well…I'll have to set him straight."

Teague gave her a fierce hug, picking her up off her feet and shaking her. A tiny giggle slipped from her lips and he kissed the top of her head. "Come on. Let's go."

As they walked to the helicopter pad, Hayley held tight to his arm. This wasn't the way he wanted their holiday to end, but he couldn't help but wonder if it might finally breach the last wall between them. Hayley needed him right now, needed his strength and his counsel. He'd help her through this hard time and perhaps they'd come out better for it on the other side.

7

TEAGUE GLANCED UP from the newspaper he was reading as Hayley approached. She'd left him in the hospital waiting room nearly an hour ago. With a soft sigh, she sat down beside him, glad for a break from the endless conversations with doctors and nurses.

They'd arrived at the hospital and she'd gone directly into a meeting with Harry's doctors. Teague had asked if she wanted him there for support, but Hayley had prepared herself to deal with the crisis on her own during the flight to Brisbane.

In truth, Hayley knew Teague had his own opinions about her grandfather, none of them very good. He thought Harry was a cranky old bastard who seemed to take delight in making Hayley miserable. Teague would always stand up for her first, especially against Harry. And now was the time to avoid conflict at all costs.

"He's refusing an IV," Hayley finally said. "And he won't even consider surgery."

Teague took her hand. "He'll change his mind once he gets tired of lying in that bed."

She tried to control the tremble in her voice, but then

realized it didn't matter. She was talking to Teague. He could handle her emotions. He'd seen plenty of them over the past few weeks. "But if he doesn't get enough fluids, then they can't do surgery. And if he doesn't have surgery, he won't walk again. I don't know what to do. He won't listen to me."

"Would you like me to talk to him?"

"No! He'd probably break the other hip trying to chase you out of the room. They're bringing in a counselor to talk to him later today. They asked that I get some of his things from home. They think if he has some reminders of his life at Wallaroo, he'll be more apt to want to get well so he can return home." She turned to him. "I don't want to leave. I—I made a list and I was hoping you could go to Wallaroo and pick up a few things." She handed him the piece of paper.

"I'll do that," Teague said, taking the list from her. "But first, why don't we get you settled in a hotel, somewhere close by."

Hayley shook her head. "No, I'm going to stay here. They have a small room for family members. There's a bed if I need to sleep. I think I should try to talk to Harry again later tonight after the counselor leaves."

"Why is he doing this?"

"He told the doctor that he's finished living. He's done. If he can't ride a horse without falling off, then he's pretty useless on a cattle station."

"He's feeling sorry for himself."

"Well, he has good reason. Wallaroo isn't what it used to be. I think all of the troubles at the station might come from this anger of his. He's mad at his body, that it doesn't work the way it should, that he can't spend twelve hours in the saddle, seven days a week. He's seventy-five years old. What does he expect?"

"I suppose I can sympathize. I know I'd be pissed off with the world if I were stuck in that hospital bed. He's always been so independent and now he needs help. Harry Fraser has never needed another human being in his life."

Hayley leaned over and rested her head on Teague's shoulder. "I often wonder whether he would have been different had my grandmother lived. I never knew her, but he has a picture of her next to his bed."

"How did your grandmother die?"

"Complications after childbirth," Hayley replied. "Three days after my father was born. She gave birth on Wallaroo and I guess everything was fine until a couple days later. She got sick and by the time they got her to the hospital, it was too late." Hayley paused. "I can see why Harry hates hospitals. Can you blame him?"

"How come you never told me that story?"

"I didn't know it until just a few years ago. I asked Daisy Willey and she told me." She sighed. "Maybe Harry would have had a happy life and they'd have moved off the station in their retirement and lived in a cottage on the ocean. Or maybe they would have gone to the city, like your parents did."

She glanced at the clock on the wall. It was already three in the afternoon. Teague needed to leave for the airport soon or he'd be spending the night. "You should go. You're not going to make it to Kerry Creek before sunset if you don't leave now."

"I'm going to stay. I'll fly to Wallaroo tomorrow morning. We'll get some dinner and I'll get a room. That way, you could rest for a while before coming back here."

"No, you should go," Hayley insisted. "You've been away from work for three days. And you'll be back tomorrow with Harry's things, remember?"

Though it was generous of Teague to offer to stay, Hayley felt it was her duty to deal with Harry. He was her family, her responsibility. Besides, it felt good to do something. She'd been all but useless to Harry for most of her life. Now she could help him get through this, help him get well.

Teague pulled her hand up to his lips and kissed her fingertips. "Walk me down to the door?"

"I should—"

"Harry isn't going anywhere. He'll be fine." Teague stood, then drew Hayley up beside him. They headed toward the lift and once inside, Teague gathered her into his arms and kissed her softly. She held on as tightly as she could, hoping to draw some strength from him.

He always knew exactly the thing to make her feel better, to lift her spirits. She closed her eyes as he gently smoothed his hand over her hair, her face nuzzled into his chest. A memory of her childhood flickered in her mind. Her mother had often done that when Hayley had awoken from a bad dream, soothing her fears until she'd fallen back asleep.

But this wasn't a bad dream. It was bad reality. She

had no one to blame but herself for this disaster. She'd been the one to take off with Teague, leaving her grandfather to fend for himself. If she'd been watching over him at Wallaroo, he would never have gotten on a horse and ridden to Kerry Creek.

Hayley couldn't believe they'd run out of time. She wanted some of those years back, years that she could have used to get to know her grandfather better. She barely remembered her parents, had never known her grandmother and she couldn't face losing the last member of her family. Without Harry, she'd be utterly alone in the world.

The doors opened and they stepped out into the lobby of the hospital. She sat down while Teague walked to the reception desk to call a taxi.

If Harry agreed to the surgery, she was willing to deal with all the consequences. There would be a long rehabilitation, but the promise of going home might tempt him to work harder. And he would go back to Wallaroo, to live out his days on the station he loved.

Harry wouldn't sell. He had never looked at his land as a financial asset. It was part of his family heritage, something that didn't have a monetary value. In truth, the station was part of who she was, too. Whether she wanted to admit it or not, the land she'd played on as an adolescent was more a parent to her than Harry had been.

He'd always lived his life by his own rules and he had a right to make his own choices. Hayley closed her eyes. Maybe she ought to respect Harry's wishes now and let him do as he wanted—no IV, no surgery. Who was she to stop him? If he wanted this to be the end, then maybe it should be, on his own terms.

But she didn't want to lose him—not yet. Hayley had always held out hope that she'd find a way to make him love her. When she'd run away, she'd wanted him to come looking for her, praying he'd show that he really did care. But Harry had never once tried to find her. And when Teague had tried, Harry had stood in his way.

Grandparents were supposed to love their grandchildren. Yet she'd managed to get the world's worst set of grandparents. Three were long gone, her mother's parents unknown to her and her grandmother just a photo beside Harry's bed. And then Harry, who'd never come close to the kindly, indulgent old folks she'd seen on the telly.

"Hayley?"

Startled out of her thoughts, she turned to find Teague standing in front of her. "Yes?"

"The taxi's outside," he said. "I have to go."

She quickly rose, then pushed up onto her toes and kissed his cheek. "Thank you," she said. "For bringing me here. And for the holiday. With the rush to leave the resort, I never told you how much fun I had."

He grinned. "We're going to do it again. Remember? You're making the plans."

"And thank you for going to get Harry's things from Wallaroo. I feel like you give so much to me and—"

"Don't," he warned. "Don't even say it. If I didn't want to be here, I wouldn't be here. It's as simple as that."

"You're a good friend, Teague," she said. "My only

true friend." She suddenly wanted to drag him off to a dark corner and lose herself in a frantic seduction, anything to take her mind off her troubles. But the distraction wouldn't last. Harry would still be lying in a hospital bed once they were through.

They walked outside and stopped next to the waiting cab. "I've been thinking," Hayley said. "I wonder if Harry is the way he is because he's been alone for so long. Because he lost the one person he loved in the whole world."

"I think Harry was born mean."

"But what would you do if you lost the person you loved?" Hayley asked. "I mean, not if she went away. But if she suddenly died? Wouldn't you turn bitter like Harry did?"

He considered her question for a long time, lazily playing with her fingers as he did. "I can't believe I'm going to say this, but, yeah, maybe I would. I guess it does explain his behavior a little better. He had his reasons."

"He did," Hayley agreed.

Teague reached for the door of the taxi. "I'll see you tomorrow morning," he said. "Ring my satellite phone if you need anything. In fact, call me later and let me know how things are going."

"I will."

Teague pulled her toward him, his mouth coming down on hers in a deep and stirring kiss. Hayley felt her legs go weak and she clutched at his shirt to maintain her balance. When he finally drew back, she remained limp in his arms, her eyes closed. Just hours ago, she would have tumbled him into their comfortable bed at the resort. Now, he was leaving.

When she looked up, he smiled softly at her. "Love you," he murmured.

"I love you," she replied, the words coming without a trace of hesitation.

With that, he let go of her, the impact of his revelation slowly sinking in and stealing her breath away. He jumped into the taxi and then gave her a wave as it drove off.

Hayley fought the urge to run after him, to demand an explanation. What did he mean? How could he say such a thing and then leave? He loved her like a best friend loves a best friend, right? And what about her? What did she mean?

She sat down on a nearby bench, numbly staring down the driveway, a frown wrinkling her brow. Maybe he'd said it to make her feel better, to boost her spirits. Hayley swallowed hard. Or—or maybe Teague really loved her.

A shiver raced through her body and she rubbed her arms to smooth away the goose bumps. *Love*. Such a simple word, a word they'd used so many times as teenagers. But back then, they hadn't known what it meant, how deep the feelings could run, how strong the bond could be. Did they know now? Or was it still only a word with vague emotions behind it?

"Are you all right, miss?"

She looked up to see an orderly standing beside the bench, a wheelchair in front of him.

"Yes. I'm fine. Just getting a little air." Hayley drew in a deep breath, then let it go. From the moment she'd first seen Teague again in the stables at Wallaroo, she'd felt as though she were clinging to the neck of a runaway horse. She wanted to jump off, to take some time and reestablish her bearings, to clear her head and think. But if she got off, could she climb back on or would the ride suddenly be over?

She pushed to her feet, the weight of emotional exhaustion making it hard to move. Perhaps the hospital had a nice quiet psychiatric ward where she could spend the next few days sorting through her feelings.

"I'VE NEVER ASKED YOU for anything, but I need this."

"No," Callum said, shaking his head. He shoved away from his desk and began to pace the width of the room. "I can't believe you'd even ask."

Teague schooled his temper, knowing only a calm discussion would get him what he wanted. Callum could be so stubborn at times, but he was also a reasonable man. And though Teague was asking an awful lot, he hoped his brother would relent. "I'll give you whatever you want for it. You know I'm good for it. I have the practice. I'll pay you back with interest."

"That's Quinn land," Callum said.

"Harry Fraser would dispute that."

"Now you're taking Harry's side?" Callum cursed beneath his breath. "I should have known this would happen."

"She doesn't have anything to do with this," Teague said. "It's me. I'm making this request."

The door to the office swung open and Gemma

stepped inside before she noticed the two of them. "I'm sorry," she said, turning to leave.

Callum's expression softened. "No, come on in. We're done here."

Teague stood and walked to the door. "We're not done here. Could you excuse us?"

Gemma glanced at them both, then nodded and quickly made her retreat. Callum made a move for the door, but Teague blocked his way. "We're going to finish this," Teague said.

"We are finished."

"You forget that all three of us have a share in this station. You may have a larger share because you run it. But I've been providing free vet service for over a year now and that's worth something."

Callum sat down at his desk and pulled out his check register. "How much do I owe you?"

"I don't want to be paid. I want you to sell me the land at a fair price."

"I'm not selling that land," Callum insisted.

"If you don't agree, then I'm going to have to call Brody and we'll bring it to a vote. If he votes with me, then you lose."

Since his father had moved off the station and turned the operation over to Callum, he'd given his sons an equal vote in any major decisions that had to be made regarding their birthright. Though Brody might side with Callum, the threat of bringing any subject to a vote underscored the serious nature of Teague's request.

"If there was one thing you could do to make Gemma's life happier, you'd do it, right?"

"Yes," Callum said.

"And I'd do the same for Hayley. That's why I need to give her grandfather that land. I wouldn't ask if it wasn't really important. You'll need to trust me on this, Cal. It will all work out in the end."

Callum gave Teague a shrewd look. "You're not a stupid bloke. But I honestly think you're being suckered into this."

"You know when it comes to the land, we each own a third. That piece doesn't even come close to a third. I'll take it and you can have the rest of my share."

"You're mad. You're willing to give up everything for a few hundred acres and a water bore?"

"I am," Teague replied.

Callum shook his head. "No. I'm not going to let you do that." He slowly closed the check register. "I'll sell you the land. But for the next five years, anything comes to a vote, you vote with me."

Teague smiled. "Thank you. This will all turn out in the end. I promise."

"I'm going to hold you to that promise," Callum warned. "Now, get the hell out of my office. And tell Gemma she can come in."

Teague had one more request and knew it wouldn't go over very well. "If it's possible, I'd like the agreement today. Before I head to Brisbane."

"Today? Why today?"

"Because I need it today." He glanced at his watch.

"In the next hour or two would be good." Teague walked to the door, then turned and sent Callum a grateful smile. "Thanks, Cal. I owe you. Free vet services for the next fifty years."

"That would about cover it," Callum said. "As long as you throw in ownership of the plane, too."

Teague left the office and climbed the stairs to his bedroom. He'd have to pack for at least a week if he expected to run his part of the practice out of Brisbane and spend his nights with Hayley. Though he'd use extra fuel flying back and forth, he could extend his workday by at least three or four hours by landing in Brisbane at the end of the day, taking advantage of the illuminated runways there.

He wasn't the kind of guy who folded when times got tough. And he knew how fragile Hayley could be when she felt as if she'd been deserted. The deal he'd made to give Harry the land would make her smile. And it might change Harry's mind about checking out early. Teague gathered some clean clothes from the pile Mary had put on the end of his bed and tossed them into a duffel bag.

He'd gotten up at sunrise and driven over to Wallaroo. He'd felt a bit strange going through Harry's belongings, but he'd found everything on Hayley's list—a flannel robe, a battered stockman's hat, a framed photo of Harry with Wallaroo's prize bull and a key chain with a lucky rabbit's foot.

He'd thought about taking the photo of Hayley's grandmother, then realized why Hayley hadn't put it on the list. Maybe Harry was ready to be with her again and the photo would only remind him of that. Teague couldn't imagine how any of the other things would be important to Harry, but then, he didn't know Hayley's grandfather.

He'd also ventured into Hayley's room and packed some of her clothes into one of her designer bags. Teague had actually enjoyed picking through *her* things, remembering when she'd worn each item of clothing, inhaling the scent of her perfume and her shampoo, flipping through some of the scripts she'd brought along.

He hadn't spoken to Hayley last night and was left to assume she was all right. Sleep had been impossible, his thoughts rewinding to their time at the resort. It seemed as if their holiday was weeks ago, even though they'd just left the island the day before.

A knock sounded on his door and he turned to find Gemma standing in the hallway. "Hi," she said. "I heard about Hayley's grandfather." She held up a paper bag. "Mary and I baked some biscuits. Shortbread. I know she probably won't have time to eat, so… It's not much, I know."

Teague crossed the room and took the bag. "Thanks. I'm sure she'll appreciate it."

"Tell her I hope everything turns out well. And if she needs anything, she should call."

"I will."

"My grandfather passed on last year. I used to spend summers with him. He was such a kind man, always looking out for me. I was devastated. I cried for days."

"Hayley and her grandfather aren't really close," Teague said.

"But I thought she grew up on the station."

"She did. But—"

"No need to explain," Gemma said, holding up her hand. "And tell her I hope we have a chance to see each other again before I go home."

"You're going home?" Teague asked.

"I'm almost done with my work. I'm needed in Dublin."

"You wouldn't have to leave," Teague said. "I know Cal enjoys having you here. And you haven't learned to ride yet."

Gemma giggled. "I've tried. But I'm fairly certain that, even if I stayed for a year, I'd never be much good at it."

"A year? That would be about enough time," he said. Teague studied her for a long moment, wondering how much he ought to say, then realized that Callum could probably use as much help as he could get. "My brother has spent his whole life working this station. There's no one who works harder than he does to make sure this place turns a profit. He's not the most romantic guy in the world, or the smoothest, but he has a lot of good qualities."

"You don't have to—"

"I do, because I know Cal never would. He's a pretty humble guy. But he's steady and loyal and—" Teague chuckled. "And I'm making him sound like the family dog."

"I understand what you're saying. And I do appreciate all his fine qualities. It's just that…well, it would be a huge thing for me to leave my life in Ireland behind. And there's no question that I'd have to do that if we were to be together." She paused. "And he hasn't asked me to stay."

Teague nodded. He wasn't going to try to sell Gemma on life at the station. It wasn't easy and she and Cal would have to love each other deeply in order to make it work. His mother hadn't been able to take it, Hayley had left and even Brody and Payton had escaped to the city.

"Well, I'll leave you to your packing," Gemma said. "Enjoy the biscuits."

Teague nodded. How odd was it that all three of the Quinn brothers now had women in their lives? And that all three of them risked losing those women. Payton and Gemma were foreigners and would probably be returning home soon. And Hayley? He figured he still had a shot with her.

They, at least, lived on the same continent.

TEAGUE SAT ACROSS the table from Hayley, watching as she picked at the pasta salad he'd brought her for dinner. Shadows smudged the skin below her eyes, betraying her lack of sleep the previous night.

"You're not staying at the hospital tonight," Teague said. "I've got a room. After you're finished eating, I'm taking you with me and you're going to get some rest."

Hayley nodded and sighed. "All right." She glanced around the hospital cafeteria. "Do you think anyone would be bothered if I crawled over the table and curled up in your lap?"

Teague grinned. "That lady behind the cash register looks strong enough to toss us both out."

"I want to kiss you for an hour or two," she said, stifling a yawn. "And then I want to pull the covers over my head and sleep for a year."

"How is Harry?"

She shrugged. "Still stubborn. But I think the things you brought him made an impact. He was wearing his hat when I left his room. And I heard him joking with one of the nurses and Harry never jokes. I think they're flirting with him. The counselor was in again today and has made some progress. If Harry agrees, they'll do his surgery tomorrow morning."

"I have something else for you," Teague said. "Actually, for Harry. But you can give it to him." He reached into his jacket pocket and withdrew an envelope, holding it out to her.

"What is it?"

"An agreement to deed the land over to me. And another to transfer it from me to Harry. It's his."

Hayley gasped, her eyes suddenly wide. "You did this for Harry?"

"I did it for you," Teague said. "And Harry. Maybe it will help."

"Oh, it will," she said, excitement filling her voice. "The court fight was weighing on his mind and this makes it all so simple. Thank you." Hayley glanced down at her uneaten dinner and pushed it aside. "I want to go tell him. Now."

"Let's go," Teague said.

They rode the lift up to Harry's floor, but before they got to the room, Hayley took Teague's hand and pulled him into through a doorway in the middle of the hall. Three cots lined the walls of the darkened room. This was obviously where Hayley had slept the night before.

She pressed him back against the closed door, his body blocking the window and their only source of light. Then she wrapped her arms around his neck and kissed him, deeply and desperately. Her need to touch him seemed frantic and she pulled at the buttons of his shirt until she'd undone them all.

He tipped his head back as she smoothed her hands over his chest. Her touch set his body on fire, every nerve tingling with anticipation. His cock grew hard almost immediately.

Hayley nuzzled his chest. "I missed you," she murmured.

Teague chuckled as she trailed kisses along his collarbone. "It's been less than twenty-four hours."

"It seemed like days," she said. "Weeks."

"Maybe because we'd spent the previous three days in bed."

"We weren't in bed the whole time. We did walk on the beach and eat."

"But it was pretty much a sexfest."

She looked up at him, grinning. "I like that. A sexfest. I think we should have another one of those."

"I know exactly where to find one. My hotel room. Fifteen minutes."

She quickly buttoned his shirt. "Let me go give Harry

the news and then we can leave." She reached down and ran her fingers along the front of his jeans. "You can stay here if you'd like. Until you…calm down. I'll only be a few minutes." She pulled the envelope out of her pocket. "Harry is going to be so surprised."

Hayley slipped out of the room and Teague sat down on the edge of the cot. He drew a deep breath, trying to douse the fire that raged inside him. Would his desire for her ever fade? Perhaps a long-distance relationship would be the perfect thing for them. All that time apart for their need to increase and then coming together again for an explosion of lust.

Yet, there was something to be said for the everyday events, the tiny things in life they could share if they lived together. He could touch her and kiss her whenever he chose. He could read her moods and soothe her worries. They could build a real life, together, maybe have a family.

Teague wanted to believe it would happen that way. Maybe not tomorrow or even next year, but someday he and Hayley would be together for good. He pushed to his feet and opened the door, stepping out into the brightly lit hallway.

He stood outside Harry's room, trying to hear the conversation inside. There was no shouting, which was a positive sign. Maybe this scheme of his would work.

A few minutes later, Hayley emerged, a smile on her face. Teague breathed a silent sigh of relief. She was happy. That was all he cared about.

"How did it go?"

"Good," she said. "We had a really nice talk." Hayley shook her head in disbelief. "He said he wanted me to be happy. And he said he'd go ahead with the surgery." She reached up and pressed her palm to Teague's chest, right over his heart, her eyes fixed on the spot. They stood that way for a long time, silent, the heat of her fingers warming his blood. "And he'd like to see you."

"Me?"

She nodded then glanced up at him. "Try to be nice."

Teague gave her hand a squeeze, then reached for the door. He wasn't quite sure what to expect. Was Harry going to throw the agreement back in his face? Or was he going to accept the land graciously?

The room was dimly lit, the blinds on the window turned down. Teague was shocked by Harry's appearance. He was immobilized by traction, ropes and slings and pulleys keeping his right leg at an angle. The man had always seemed so powerful. But he looked so small in the big bed, his skin pale, his beard grizzled.

"Hello, Mr. Fraser."

"Quinn," he said. He pointed to the chair beside the bed, but Teague shook his head. "I'm good."

"Hayley showed me this." He waved the paper. "Is it real?"

Teague nodded. "Yeah. My brother gave me the land and I'm giving it to you."

"Does your brother know about this?"

"Yes. As soon as you're out of here, we'll get all the papers signed and make it official. But it's yours."

"Why are you doing this?"

"For Hayley."

"You expect me to turn her over to you because you gave me the land?"

Teague laughed. "Jaysus, Harry, she's not a horse. You can't trade her like a piece of property. I did this because I thought it might keep your arse alive. That's what Hayley wants and I want what she wants."

Harry scowled. "Are you in love with her?"

"Yes," Teague said. "I have been since I was a kid."

"So, I guess you figure once I leave this world, she'll get everything and you'll waltz right in and share in the wealth?"

Teague cursed beneath his breath. "Go to hell, Harry. I don't give a shit about Wallaroo. But after all you've put Hayley through, the mess you made of her childhood, I think she deserves the place after you depart this life. Although, I don't expect you'll be dying anytime soon since it's your goal to make her as miserable as possible."

"I don't want that," Harry said. He went silent for a long time, turning his head away from Teague to look out the window. "I know I didn't do well by her. But I didn't know how to take care of her any more than I knew how to care for my own son."

"It's not that hard to love her," Teague said. "I fell in love with her the very first time I saw her."

"I guess it's my fault, then. I never knew what to say to her. Hell, I drove her father off Wallaroo and I figured she wouldn't have any interest in sticking around, either. She proved my point when she ran away."

"I don't know why, but she does care about you."

Harry shifted, wincing as he tried to sit up a little straighter. "They have me so shot full of pain medicine, I'm not sure what I'm saying, but I'm going to say it anyway. If I don't make it through the surgery, I want you to watch over her. I may have had my troubles with your father and your brother, but you seem like a decent sort, Quinn. And Hayley likes you."

"I think she does," Teague said. "But you are going to make it through this operation. And then you'll go somewhere where they'll get you walking again. And then you'll go home to Wallaroo. And I'm going to see that you're a lot nicer to Hayley from now on."

"You seem pretty damn sure of yourself," Harry said.

"I am. And if you don't try to make that happen, then you and I are going to have a problem."

"Good enough," he said. "Then I guess we have an understanding?"

"We do," Teague said.

"Now get the hell out of my room and let me sleep," Harry ordered.

Teague turned and walked to the door, smiling to himself as he stepped into the hallway. Hayley was waiting for him outside the door. He wrapped his arm around her shoulders and walked with her toward the lift. "It went well. We had a nice talk. Now let's get out of here."

They found Teague's rental in the car park. Teague pulled the door open for Hayley, then circled around to the driver's side. The hotel was less than a mile away, but Hayley wasn't in the mood to wait. She ran her hand along his thigh as he turned onto the street, then slid it in between his legs.

He grabbed her wrist to stop her from going farther, but she just smiled and ignored him. By the time they reached the hotel, he was completely aroused, his erection straining at the fabric of his jeans.

When they pulled in to the hotel car park, Teague retrieved his jacket from the rear seat and held it over his groin as he and Hayley strolled into the lobby. He glanced over to see a satisfied grin on her face. "Thank you," Teague said. "I always appreciate walking around like this. It makes me look like a pervert."

They rode the lift in silence. When he opened the room door and stepped aside, Hayley trailed her fingers across the front of his jeans as she walked past him.

The moment the door closed, she began undressing him. He reached for her shirt, but she brushed his hands away. Teague decided to let her have her way with him, curious how far she would go to pleasure him.

By the time she had him stripped naked, he really didn't care what she did. The feel of her fingers wrapped around his shaft was enough to bring him to the edge. But Hayley had other plans. She kissed a trail from his mouth to his chest and then lower.

He felt oddly vulnerable. She was still dressed and he was naked. But the moment her mouth closed over him, he realized that this situation was fantasy material. She was in control, seducing him, and he could simply relax and enjoy the ride.

It hadn't taken Hayley long to learn what he liked,

exactly what stoked his desire. They'd had plenty of practice during their holiday. Teague drew in a deep breath and held it, her tongue sending him closer to release. But she read the signs and slowed her pace, smoothing her hands over his belly as she pulled back.

He was so hard, he wasn't sure he could be any more aroused. But then, Hayley stood. Her gaze fixed on his, she slowly stripped out of her clothes, as if performing for him. The striptease was even more intriguing than physical contact.

He reached for her, but she evaded his grasp. And when she was completely undressed, she didn't return to touching him. Instead, she ran her hands over her own body. Teague groaned, aching to touch her but still caught up in the game she was playing. But when she slipped her fingers between her legs, he growled softly and grasped her waist with his hands.

Picking her up off her feet, Teague wrapped her legs around him, holding tight to her hips. Her lips found his and she twisted her fingers through his hair as she kissed him. Slowly, Teague entered her, a surge of desire washing over him. And when he was buried deep, Hayley sighed softly, a satisfied smile curling her lips. "Oh, don't move. That feels so good," she said breathlessly.

"I have to move," he said.

"No, you don't."

"Let me move," he said.

She shifted above him and he gasped. Maybe he didn't need to move. But the pleasure was too strong to deny. Teague held her tight as he slowly withdrew, then drove forward again. She whispered his name, her lips soft against his ear.

This was all he needed, Teague thought. The only thing in his life he couldn't do without. Her body was the perfect match for his, her heart and her soul the prize he wanted to possess. And though he hoped to spend a lifetime with her, Teague knew he'd be happy with one more day and the night that followed.

8

THE SKY WAS GRAY and overcast as the plane flew low over the outback landscape. Hayley had thought about canceling the trip, leaving it for a sunnier day, but then decided that the weather matched her mood. It had been nearly a week since she'd last smiled, the evening after Harry's surgery, when she'd sat by her grandfather's bed and told him that she loved him.

Hayley looked down at the urn on her lap, running her hands over the cool ceramic surface. The numbness had begun to wear off and reality had set in. Harry was gone.

He'd written detailed plans before going into surgery, scribbling everything he wanted her to know on a small scrap of paper. She'd found it a day later, after the hospital had returned his belongings. No funeral, no mourning, scatter his ashes over Wallaroo.

His death had been unexpected. He'd survived the surgery and had been making plans to enter a rehabilitation center. She'd said good-night to him that evening, happy that things had gone so well, and the next morning, when she'd arrived at the hospital, the staff had told her Harry had passed away during the night.

It had been a quiet death, in his sleep, and though the doctors wanted to give her all the details and the cause, Hayley really didn't want to listen. She knew why Harry had died. He'd done as she had asked, and then chosen his own time, on his own terms. In the end, Hayley was grateful that he never had to know a long, debilitating illness.

She had wanted to grieve for him, but she knew Harry wouldn't approve. There had been tears, but after the tears had come comfort in knowing that Harry's spirit would always live on at Wallaroo, in the beautiful sunsets and wide, sweeping vistas, in the shimmer of light off the slow-moving creeks and in the soft breeze that brought the rain.

"This looks like a nice spot," Teague said. "With the creek and that outcropping right there. It's very peaceful."

"It is," Hayley said. "What should I do?"

"Open the window and take the top off once you're holding the urn outside. Then tip it toward the tail of the plane."

Hayley slid the window open. "Goodbye, Harry." She followed Teague's instructions and watched as the cloud of ashes flew past the plane and drifted down to the ground. It was difficult to believe Harry wouldn't be there when they got to the house, sitting on the porch, watching over his property. She'd never have to cook him supper or pick up after him again. She'd never have to listen to him complain.

Hayley had been so young when her parents had died that she barely remembered feeling anything then. One day, they were there and the next day they weren't. The minister had told her to be brave. The people at the funeral home had patted her on the head and whispered behind her back. And though she felt the loss, she hadn't been old enough to understand the true impact it would have on her life.

"He was all I had left," Hayley said.

"You have me." Teague reached for her hand and gave it a squeeze. "Cal asked if I'd bring you over for dinner tonight. Gemma is going to be leaving soon and she wanted to say goodbye."

Hayley smiled weakly. "I can't. I'd really rather go home. I've got a lot to do."

"Nothing that can't wait," he said.

"I have to make some decisions. I have to get back to Sydney. I'm supposed to fly to Los Angeles next week. And I'm due at the studio right after that to finish taping *Castle Cove.*"

"So you're going to leave?"

"I don't have much choice," Hayley said.

"The station is yours now. You've watched Harry run it. You could do the same. You could raise horses, give the Quinns some competition. And you've got free vet services. There are plenty of station owners who'd kill for that."

"I can't live out here alone," she said.

"You wouldn't be alone," Teague replied. "I'd be here. I could move my things over and come and go from Wallaroo."

Hayley felt her cheeks warm. Was this a marriage

proposal or a business proposal? "And what would we be?"

"Whatever you wanted us to be," he said. "Friends? Lovers? Partners? Roommates?"

She turned away, her pulse racing at the thought of accepting his offer. She could have Teague with her for as long as she wanted. Or as long as he wanted, whichever came first. Though the thought of losing him terrified her, it wasn't half as bad as the thought of never having him in the first place.

"I know what you're thinking," Teague said. "Where's the parachute? I gotta get out of this plane."

Hayley couldn't help but laugh. "You planned this so I couldn't escape?"

"It looks that way. You don't have to give me an answer now, Hayley. But at least consider the option."

"Good. Because I don't have an answer now," she replied.

"But you'll think about it?"

Hayley nodded. It was the least she could do. Besides, it was a plan worth examining. She could imagine a life on Wallaroo with Teague. It would be simple, but satisfying. She could also picture her life in Sydney, her career, making movies and traveling the world.

If she decided not to stay, the sale of the station would provide her with the kind of lifelong security she'd always wanted. She could take the time to choose good projects, to build a film career slowly and carefully. And she'd never have to depend on another person for her day-to-day existence.

But Teague wouldn't understand that reason, her need to be able to survive without help from anyone. He seemed happy to have her dependent on him, to provide for her and make sure her life was easy.

They landed on the airstrip on Wallaroo, then rode to the house in Hayley's car. They bumped along the rough dirt track, Teague bracing his hand on the dash. "If you're going to live on Wallaroo, you're going to need a better way to get around. The suspension on this thing will last about a week."

"Right," she said softly. As she focused on the road ahead, she thought about the other changes she'd have to make. She'd have to sell her place in Sydney, give up acting and walk away from the life she'd built for herself. To live in the middle of nowhere.

But here, on the station, she would have love. And no matter how she turned it over in her head, there was no possible way she could have both.

When they reached the house, Hayley stopped the car and got out. But she couldn't bring herself to go inside. She'd spent the past week wandering around the station, cleaning the stables and the yard, taking long rides in the outback with Molly, sitting on the porch and memorizing her lines for the next three episodes of *Castle Cove*. She'd avoided the house as much as possible, knowing she'd have to face sorting through Harry's things.

Teague had been occupied with work and had only spent a few nights with her, sleeping by her side while she passed the night wide-awake and restless, her mind a jumble of disparate thoughts.

"I can't," she said, staring at the house. "I can't go inside. Not now. It's too sad."

He pulled her along, holding tight to her hand. "We don't have to go inside," he said. "Let's ride out to the shack. We haven't been there for a while. It'll be fun."

Hayley nodded and they walked toward the stables. She sat on a bale of straw as Teague saddled Molly. When he was finished, he gave her a knee up and then settled himself behind her. He gave Molly a gentle kick and they started out into the gray daylight.

"When I go home to Sydney, I want you to take Molly to Kerry Creek. Find someone to ride her every day."

"I can do that," Teague said.

She sank against him and closed her eyes. Exhaustion seemed to descend on her all at once, the gentle gait of the horse lulling her toward sleep. Everything seemed so right when Teague was with her. He was strong when she couldn't be and he made her laugh when she felt gloomy. He talked to her when she needed an opinion and listened when she didn't.

From the moment she'd seen him standing outside Molly's stall, Hayley had known what she was risking. And now, she was left to deal with the consequences of falling in love with Teague all over again. Only this time, she'd be the one to walk away and leave him behind.

Somehow, that didn't make her decision easier. It made the prospect of leaving almost impossible to bear.

"I'M NOT QUITE SURE why I'm here," Teague said, looking around the interior of the solicitor's office. Both he and Hayley had been summoned to Brisbane for the reading of Harry's will. Teague had assumed that it had to do with the land he'd given Harry.

The solicitor cleared his throat as he rearranged the stacks of files on his desk. "Since both you and Miss Fraser are mentioned in the will, it's customary."

Teague frowned. "I'm in the will? How can that be?"

"Harry made some last-minute changes. He called me over to the hospital the morning of his surgery so he could sign the new addendum."

"Let me guess. He left me the Quinn land that I gave to him."

"No," the solicitor said. "He left you half of Wallaroo."

Both Teague and Hayley gasped at the same time, then looked at each other. "Say that again," Teague murmured.

"You two are to share ownership in the station. Fifty-fifty. Harry decided if his granddaughter did not want to keep the station, then it should go to the Quinns. You are both required to live on the station for at least six months out of the year or you will forfeit your right to ownership. After ten years, if you both agree to sell, then you will split the profits from the sale fifty-fifty. If there is no agreement to sell, then this arrangement remains in force."

"But I can't live on the station," Hayley said. "I have a career in Sydney."

"Then I'm afraid the station will go to the Quinns, as long as Mr. Quinn is following the residency clause. Are you willing to live on Wallaroo?"

"Yes," Teague said.

"Of course he is," Hayley said. "It's perfect. The Quinns have always wanted Wallaroo. And now they have it." She turned to Teague. "What kind of deal did you make with him? Did you talk him into this?"

"No!" Teague said. "I'm as surprised as you are."

"You're sure you didn't figure out some way to force the issue, to make me stay on Wallaroo? Because this seems awfully suspicious to me."

"Well, it seems downright crazy to me. Harry asked me to take care of you, but I never thought—"

"And what did you say?" she demanded. "Did you tell him you would?"

"Of course."

"See. That's what it was. He assumed you'd marry me and we'd live happily ever after on Wallaroo."

"Well, it's not such a bad idea," Teague said. "Didn't you say you'd always dreamed we'd have a station together, with horses?"

"I was a kid," Hayley said. "And it was just a stupid dream. I have a life of my own now. I don't need you making decisions for me."

"Would you two like a moment alone?" the solicitor asked.

"No!" Hayley said.

"Yes," Teague answered.

The solicitor got up and Hayley shook her head. "Why do you listen to him and not to me?"

When the solicitor shut the office door behind him, Hayley turned to Teague. "You can't force me to live on Wallaroo."

"I'm not forcing you to do anything, Hayley. This was Harry's deal, not mine. But I can understand his thinking. Wallaroo has been in your family for years. He didn't want to see it sold. And you shouldn't, either. It's part of your heritage."

"I make my own decisions about my life. Not you, not Harry, me."

"So you don't want to be with me?"

"Not because of some scheme you and Harry cooked up," she said.

"I see." Teague shrugged. Hell, there were times when Hayley's ability to reason flew right out the window. Instead of thinking things through, she reacted. They could make this arrangement work. Teague could run the station and she could come and go as she pleased. He wouldn't hold her to the residency clause— at least not down to the letter.

But if he did decide to enforce the rules, he'd have her for six months out of the year. If he couldn't convince her they belonged together given that amount of time, then maybe they didn't belong together at all.

"If you don't like the terms, then don't follow them."

"I'd lose my share of Wallaroo," she said.

"You hate Wallaroo."

"I don't hate it. I just never appreciated it until I came back this last time."

"What do you want me to do?"

"Give me your half," she demanded. "That's the only fair thing to do."

"No," Teague said. "You aren't prepared to run it

alone. And it's the perfect place to raise horses. What land we don't use for that, we can lease to Callum for cattle."

"You have it all planned out, don't you? This plays right into your hand. Why don't we both agree to break the rules and sell it. You can come to Sydney with me and start a practice there." She raised her brow. "How about that scheme? Now you have to turn *your* life upside down for me."

"Would that make you happy?" Teague asked. "Would that mean we could spend the rest of our lives together?" He waited for her answer, knowing it wouldn't come. The question actually seemed to make her even angrier.

Had he really expected the fairy tale to last forever? Everything had been going so well for them, beyond Harry's passing. Hayley had been quiet and thoughtful, though a bit confused. But here was the Hayley he'd always known. Scrappy and opinionated, a girl who didn't let anyone push her around. Until she was backed into a corner. Then she clawed like a tiger to escape.

"I'm going to fight this in the courts," Hayley said, snatching up her bag and getting to her feet.

"Great!" Teague replied. "Now that one feud is finally over, we'll start another one."

"Tell your solicitor that he will be hearing from mine," she said as she strode to the door.

"How are you going to get home?" he shouted. "It's a long walk."

Hayley slowly turned. "I am perfectly capable of getting to Wallaroo on my own. I see you share Harry's rather low opinion of my intelligence. You two should have made friends long ago. You're so much alike."

She yanked on the door. At first, it didn't open, and when it did, it hit her on the head. Teague winced, jumping to his feet to help her. But Hayley warned him off, waving her finger at him.

Teague sat down in the chair, cursing softly as she slammed the door behind her. A few moments later, the solicitor returned, a file folder clutched in his hands. "I suspected she might be upset," he murmured as he took his place behind his desk. "These last-minute changes are always a problem. But the doctors assured me that Harry was of sound mind and all the necessary signatures were made. If there is a lawsuit, I'd be happy to testify."

"I don't think that will be necessary," Teague said. He stood and held out his hand. "Thank you. I'll be in touch."

Teague half expected Hayley to be waiting in the reception area, but when he got there, she was gone. Her behavior wasn't surprising. He'd been expecting it for some time. It was Hayley's way of coping when she felt herself growing too close to someone, depending too much on another human being.

She'd done it when they were teenagers, refusing to speak to him for days after some silly fight. He'd always figured that must be the way all girls behaved. But now he saw it for what it was—a defense mechanism. It probably would have come earlier had her grandfather's death not delayed her.

It was the "love you" he'd mumbled to her outside the hospital that probably set it off. Too much, too soon.

It'd seemed like the proper thing to say, considering the situation. He'd wanted to reassure her, not box her into a corner. But his declaration and then the will were enough to convince her that he expected to be a part of her future—and she had no say in the matter.

"What the hell were you thinking, Harry?" Teague muttered as he walked to the car park. Though he suspected Harry had noble motives for changing his will, it only proved that he'd never really known his granddaughter. If he had, he'd have realized she'd see the move as another attempt to control her life.

Harry had suspected Hayley wouldn't want to run the station, so he'd given half of it to a Quinn. He'd thought Hayley might sell the station, so he'd made it impossible for her to do so without a Quinn's permission. If Hayley did want to run the station, then she would have help…from a Quinn.

Harry's attempt to keep the two of them together, in at least a legal and working arrangement, may have driven them apart emotionally. But Hayley would have to see the sense in it. She had a career away from the outback. And Teague was in the perfect position to make something out of Wallaroo. If he succeeded, she would profit from it, too.

Teague walked up the stairs to the second level of the car park and searched the rows of cars for his rental. He spotted it parked at the far end, right where he'd left it. As he approached he noticed Hayley leaning against the passenger-side door, her arms crossed over her chest, an annoyed expression suffusing her pretty face.

Teague ignored her, unlocked the driver's side and got in. Two could play this game. If she wanted a ride home, she'd have to ask. He wasn't going to offer.

God, she could be so exasperating. There were times when he almost believed they'd be better off giving up on their romance and beginning a chaste friendship. She wouldn't be half so skittish and any disagreements between them could be worked out in a rational fashion.

"Are you going to get in or will I have to drive over you?"

She turned and pulled on the door handle, but the passenger side was still locked. Hayley sent him a withering glare and he pushed the button to unlock it. She got inside, looking straight ahead and refusing to speak.

"You're really beautiful when you act childish," he said.

"You don't think I have a right to be angry?"

"No. Because you've assumed things that aren't true. I didn't ask Harry to do this. I was as surprised as you were. And I understand why you're angry, but don't take it out on me."

"Why not? I'm sure you think this is a perfect solution. With the station between us, you'll have exactly what you want."

"And what is that?"

"Me," she snapped.

Teague shoved the key in the ignition and started the car. "And what's so bloody wrong with me wanting you? I happen to like spending time with you. I think you're the most beautiful woman in the entire world.

And I think we'd make a good team. We could make a success of Wallaroo, turn it into something really grand. But you've got your knickers in a twist because of the way it happened."

"I can't be tied to that station."

"It's not only the station. It's everything. You're like a mare that can't be broken." As soon as the words were out of his mouth, he realized his mistake.

"Oh, that's lovely," she retorted. "As if I should want to be tamed, so I can live with a bit in my mouth and haul your arse around all day long."

"All right, maybe that wasn't the best comparison. But there are some benefits to settling down and making a commitment."

"I don't want to talk about this right now," she said. "I would rather we pass the ride to the airport in complete silence. Can you manage that?"

He felt her pulling away and there was nothing he could do to stop it. She'd been under so much stress, the weight of Harry's injury and death bending her to the breaking point. But now, with the will, she'd cracked. The wall was back up and they'd returned to where they began.

Maybe Hayley wasn't capable of a long-term relationship. He'd always wanted to believe she was perfect, but the more time he spent with her, the more he understood the ghosts that haunted her. No matter how hard he pushed, she simply pushed back.

It would be up to her to decide if they had a future. And nothing he could say or do would change that. He just hoped he wouldn't have to spend the rest of his life waiting for her to realize she loved him…and wondering what might have been if she had.

"HAYLEY!"

Teague's voice echoed through the empty house. Hayley folded the T-shirt and tucked it into her bag. Then she bent down and picked up the sandals Teague had bought her and placed them in the plastic bag with her other shoes.

"Hayley!"

She found the letter she'd written to him and tucked it into the back pocket of her jeans. His footsteps sounded on the stairs as she closed the zipper on the tote and set it beside the bed. Then she sat down and folded her hands in her lap, knowing that the next few minutes might be more difficult than she'd ever imagined.

"Hayley?" He stepped inside her bedroom. "Didn't you hear me calling?" His gaze dropped to the bag at her feet. "What's going on?"

"I have to go," she said.

"You don't have to be back in Sydney until next week."

"My agent got me an audition for a television series. They want me in Los Angeles right away. I have to go now."

He frowned, shaking his head. "A television series? In Los Angeles?"

She nodded.

"But you're not going to do it, right? You have a job like that right here in Australia."

"This would be different. This would be a lot more money."

"Hayley, you own half this station. You don't have to worry about money anymore."

"But I can't sell my half unless you agree to sell yours. So I really don't have anything except a lot of land and no money."

"If you need help, you know I'll be there to help you. Do you need money?"

"See, there's the problem." She stood up and returned to her packing, grabbing her tote and stuffing a pair of jeans inside. "Any actress would kill for an opportunity like this."

In truth, she still hadn't decided whether it was a good idea. She was *supposed* to want a better career. Her agent had said so and she usually listened to her agent. This might open the door to American movies or at least a big role in an Australian movie.

But since she'd returned to Wallaroo after the reading of the will, she hadn't thought much about her acting career. There had been long stretches of time when it hadn't even entered her mind. If acting was her passion, wasn't she supposed be obsessed with it?

Instead, she'd spent her time wandering around the house, making a mental list of the changes that needed to be made, imagining life at Wallaroo with Teague. With so much time alone, she'd found herself fantasizing an entire existence—and she'd liked what she'd seen in her head.

"I need to find out what it's all about before I get too excited," Hayley said in an indifferent tone.

"You were going to leave without saying goodbye?"

"I wrote you a letter." She risked a glance up at him. "I want you to make sure you look after Molly. And if you need any money, call me. We should share the expenses of fixing this place up. If you don't want to do that, then just keep a tally. If we ever sell the place, you can take it out of my share."

Teague cursed softly. "You're not coming back."

"That's not true. I have to come back. I'm under contract with *Castle Cove* through September."

"I meant to Wallaroo. You're not coming back here."

"I'll visit when I can." She sat down on the edge of the bed. "When are you moving in?"

"I brought some of my stuff over today. Callum is coming later to pick me up and then I'll fly the plane over here. I can't very well get this place in shape if I don't live here."

"No. There is a lot to do."

"I figure we ought to upgrade the homestead a bit while we're looking for stock. I spoke to Cal and he's interested in leasing some of the grazing land for Kerry Creek cattle. So we should have some money to invest."

He made it sound as if she was going to be part of it all. Was that wishful thinking or did he believe he could change her mind about leaving? "That's brilliant," she muttered. "You have it all figured out."

"Not all," he said. "There are still a few pieces missing, but I'm working on those."

"I don't know when I'll be able to come to Wallaroo

again," she said. "Our production schedule is always really busy. Maybe sometime in September."

"No worries. You'll be surprised when you come the next time. I'll have this place in top shape."

Hayley drew a deep breath and flopped back on the bed, staring up at the ceiling. What did he want from her? Was she supposed to feel guilty for leaving all the work to him while she ran off and became a movie star?

Teague lay down beside her, turning to face her. He reached out and toyed with a lock of her hair. "We can make this work," he said.

"Can we?"

"Only if you want to, Hayley. Do you? If you don't, then you should get up and leave right now. Because I'm not sure I'm going to be able to say goodbye without making myself look like a damn drongo."

Hayley rolled onto her side. "Kiss me," she said, saying a silent prayer that one kiss would make everything clear in her head.

"Why? Do you expect that to change anything? I could tear all your clothes off and make love to you and you'd still leave. You decided to leave the day you got here and nothing that's happened since has made a bit of difference, has it?"

"That's not true. You don't have to be cruel."

"I'm being honest," Teague said. "We've always been honest with each other, haven't we?"

Hayley heard the anger in his voice, the bitter edge that sent daggers through her soul. Teague understood her too well. He knew exactly what was running through her mind right now, the desperate need to run away and the overwhelming temptation to stay.

He rolled over and threw his arm over his eyes. "Get the hell out of here, Hayley. You don't belong here. You never have. The same way I don't belong anywhere *but* here."

"I'm—"

"Don't. I don't need any explanations. Just go."

Hayley sat up. Bracing her hand beside his body, she leaned over and brushed a kiss across his lips. "Goodbye, Teague." When he didn't reply, she slowly stood and picked up her bags. He was still lying on the bed, his arm over his face, when she turned to take one last look.

As she walked down the stairs, she slowed her pace, waiting for him to come after her, to drag her back to the bedroom and make love to her for the rest of the afternoon. By the time she reached her car, Hayley realized he wasn't going to come. He was going to let her walk away.

Drawing a ragged breath, she tossed her bags in the rear seat and got behind the wheel. She glanced up at her bedroom window, where the breeze ruffled the plain cotton curtains. He wasn't there watching.

Hayley reached for the car door, then let her hand drop. She shoved her keys into her pocket, turned and walked toward the stable.

Molly was in her stall, munching on fresh hay. She watched Hayley with huge dark eyes, blinking as Hayley smoothed her hand over the mare's nose. "You be a good girl," she said. "Teague will take care of you now. He'll make sure you have plenty to eat and get exercise. He's good with horses and you'll like him."

Hayley's eyes swam with tears. How was it she could walk away from Teague, yet the thought of leaving Molly made her cry? She kissed Molly's muzzle, then turned and ran out of the stable.

As she approached the house, she saw Teague standing on the porch, his arm braced against one of the posts, his expression unreadable. Hayley stood next to the car, watching him. Their eyes locked for a long moment. Then she smiled and gave him a small wave.

He didn't respond. Gathering her resolve, she got into the car and started the engine, then slowly drove out of the yard. She couldn't bring herself to look in the rearview mirror. No, from now on, she couldn't focus on the past. She had to look forward. Without regrets and without doubts.

This was her life and she'd make her own decisions. And whether they were right or wrong, she was willing to live with the consequences.

9

HAYLEY HAD NEVER SEEN anything like it. Miles and miles of traffic stretched out in front of the taxi, the landscape of cars wavering in the heat from the freeway pavement. Though traffic could be slow in Sydney, the government had quickly moved to fix the problem. Here in Los Angeles, people seemed to accept it as part of the lifestyle.

The airport had been worse than the freeway. Her flight had been delayed twice. She'd been scheduled to arrive twelve hours before her audition, giving her time to settle into a hotel and get some rest. Instead, she'd arrived with just two hours to spare and had to go from the airport to the studio directly.

"How long will it take to get there?" she asked the cabdriver.

He shrugged. "Maybe hour, two, could be," he replied in a heavy accent. She glanced at his name card. Vladimir Petrosky. She'd heard that all the cabdrivers and waiters and store clerks in L.A. were aspiring actors. If that was true, she'd probably have plenty of competition.

"You call," he said. "Tell them you be late."

"I don't have a phone," Hayley replied.

He passed a mobile through the window between them. "Use mine," he said. "No problem."

Hayley pulled out the copy of her itinerary and searched for the number of the studio. When she found it, she punched the digits into the phone. A receptionist answered and put her through to the assistant producer's assistant. Who put her through to the assistant producer. Who politely informed her that the producer had another appointment in an hour and if she didn't make it, they would have to reschedule for next week.

"I'll be there," she said. Hayley handed the phone to the driver. "Is there another way? Perhaps we could get off this highway and find another route?"

"Other could be bad," Vladimir said. "You have audition, yes?"

"Yes?"

He twisted around in his seat and looked at her. "You give me producer's name and phone number, I get you there on time."

Wasn't this extortion? Not a very serious case, but an actor had to do what an actor had to do. "All right," she said. "But I'm going to write it down and leave it here on the seat. If anyone asks, you don't mention my name. Deal?"

"I not know your name," Vladimir said.

"Good, that works out well for the both of us."

True to Vladimir's word, he managed to get her to the studio in under a half hour, taking the first exit off the freeway and then winding through busy city streets.

She paid him with the cash her agent had given her, then hurried through the doors of a plain two-story building on the studio lot, dragging her bags along with her.

The receptionist pointed to a long sofa and Hayley sat down. The office was decorated with photos from the programs they produced. Like her show in Australia, this was an hour-long weekly drama. Set in an American hospital, the show had launched movie careers for three of its lead actors, so a place in the cast was considered a stepping stone to bigger things.

Bigger things, she mused. Was that really what she wanted? Her mind flashed back to the room she'd shared with Teague on the island, to the perfect solitude of their waterfront bungalow. All that seemed like a dream to her now, stuck in the middle of this noisy city with a haze of smog all around it.

She closed her eyes and pictured Teague in bed, his naked limbs twisted in the sheets, his hair rumpled. That's what she wanted. Teague, naked and aroused, his lips on hers, his hands exploring her body, making her ache with desire. She wanted to go to bed at night knowing he'd be there in the morning. She wanted to talk to him about little things she'd discovered in the course of her day. And she wanted to be assured that he would always love her, no matter what.

But wasn't that exactly what she'd walked away from? Hadn't he offered that life to her? Why was it so easy to see, now that she was miles and miles away from him? Hayley pressed her palm to her chest, trying to ease the emptiness that had settled in her heart. Though she'd tried her best to convince herself otherwise, something had changed inside her.

The thought of loving him and then losing him no longer frightened her. Anything truly important always came with risks. Her real fear was that she'd go her entire life and never find another human being who would understand her the way Teague did. Had she deliberately ignored her true feelings simply because they'd begun when she was a child?

It was so easy to consider their connection a teenage infatuation, something never meant to survive to adulthood. But it had survived. And they did still love each other. And she'd been a… "Fool," Hayley whispered.

She glanced up to see the receptionist watching her with an odd expression. "Is everything all right?"

"No," Hayley said with a groan.

"Are you going to be ill?"

Hayley shook her head. "I don't think so." She stood up. "I have to leave. Can you call me a taxi?"

"But, Miss Fraser, Mr. Wells hasn't seen you yet."

"I know. But I don't want to be seen. Tell him I'm grateful for the opportunity, but I'm not interested in doing American television. I don't want to live in America. It's too far away."

"Are you sure?"

Hayley smiled. "I am. I've never been more sure of anything in my life. Isn't that crazy? I walk away from him a few days ago and now all I can think of is getting home to be with him."

The receptionist smiled. "Oh, I understand. Love?"

"Yes!" Hayley cried. "I think it might be. And I don't want to be living here while he's there. I'm not even sure I want to be in Sydney. I mean, that's at least fifteen hours by car. Although he has a plane, so he could probably come for visits. But I don't like the idea of not seeing him every day. I think if you're in love, you should be together. Don't you?"

"Yes?"

"Exactly," Hayley said. "I need to get to the airport right away. How long will it take for a taxi?"

"I'll call right now," she offered. "It will only be a few minutes."

"That would be brilliant," Hayley replied, picking up her bags. "I think it would be best if I waited outside."

She didn't want to have to make her excuses to Mr. Wells. After all, what would she say? I'm sorry, I can't audition today because I just realized I'm still in love with my childhood sweetheart. "I'm such an idiot!" Hayley cried as she shoved open the main door and stumbled out.

She stood beneath a wide awning for five minutes before she saw a taxi approach. The car stopped in front of her and she got inside, only to find Vladimir behind the wheel. He got out and tossed her bags in the boot. "It went well? You smiling."

"No," she said as she crawled inside. "It didn't go at all. But that's all right. I've got something really good waiting for me at home."

Vladimir got behind the wheel. "Where can I take you?"

"To the airport," she said.

"Quick trip," Vladimir said. He started the meter and Hayley sat back and sighed softly. Her agent was going to be furious, but she didn't care. He'd get over it. As for her acting career in Australia, she still had obligations, but once she'd fulfilled her contract, she was free to take projects she found interesting and exciting, and not just projects that would pay the bills.

Teague had been right. She owned half the station and though it wasn't money in the bank, it was financial security. She'd always have a place to live, work that she found satisfying and the chance for a comfortable future. That was all she'd ever wanted from her acting career.

What would it feel like to leave celebrity behind? She'd never really enjoyed the notoriety that her career had brought and it wasn't something she'd miss. And perhaps, someday, someone would ask what had happened to that girl who used to play the vixen on *Castle Cove*.

They'd find her living on Wallaroo with her childhood sweetheart, raising horses—and maybe a few children, as well. Although Hayley wasn't sure about the children. How could she be a good parent when she'd never had a good example to follow? But, though she barely remembered her own parents, she did remember being loved. There had been smiles and hugs and giggles.

She let her thoughts drift, images flowing through her head, all of them comforting, happy, the pieces of her life she wanted to remember. There was no reason to always expect the worst, to be waiting for some disaster to befall her. Teague had tried to tell her that, but she hadn't listened.

The next thing Hayley knew the driver was calling out to her. She opened her eyes and realized that she'd fallen asleep. Rubbing her face, she sat up and looked around. They were at the airport again, in the same spot from which Vladimir had picked her up. "Qantas?" he asked.

"Yes," she said. She fumbled with her wallet, then withdrew the rest of the American money she'd brought along. "Here, keep the change."

He frowned. "But this is too much."

"Don't worry. I don't need it. I'm going home. And I'm not going to be leaving again anytime soon."

"IT'S GOOD GRAZING LAND," Callum said, staring out across the landscape toward the horizon. "If we have more land, we can increase the size of the mob. How many hectares do you want to lease?"

"As much as you want. I plan to start small," he said. "Maybe twenty-five mares. Good stock. We won't need a lot of grazing land. I'm hoping you'll sell me five or six Kerry Creek mares."

"I don't know if I should be helping you. You're going to be competing with us."

Teague drew a deep breath, ready to lay out his plan. "You never wanted the horse-breeding operation in the first place. I'm the one who talked you into it. Why don't you let me move the whole thing over here. You'll get your pick of stock ponies at a good price and you can concentrate on cattle."

Callum thought about the offer for a moment. "He won't go for that," Brody said, his hands folded over his saddle horn, his hat pulled low over his eyes. "Cal would never pay for anything that he could get for free."

"There's where you're wrong, little brother." Callum turned to Teague. "All right. It's a deal. I'll trade you the Kerry Creek horses for lease rights on Wallaroo grazing land."

Teague glanced over at Brody. "What's wrong with Cal?"

"Lovesick," Brody said. "Right now he'd say yes to just about anything. Gemma has turned him into a shadow of his former self."

"Not only me," Cal countered. "Look at poor Teague. We're both alone again. You're the only lucky guy in this bunch. How does that figure?" He paused. "And what the hell are you doing here with us when you have Payton waiting back at the homestead?"

"She has a serious case of jet lag. I think she's going to be sleeping for the next week," Brody said.

The three brothers turned and silently surveyed the land in front of them. Teague found it odd that three women had swept into their lives in a single week, turning their lives upside down before sweeping back out. What were the chances of that happening to one of the Quinn brothers, much less all three? Well, at least Brody's girl had come back.

"Yep, we're a pretty pathetic pair," Teague said, patting Callum on the shoulder. "Do you think it's something in the genes?"

"Must be," Brody muttered. "I have plenty in my jeans to satisfy a woman."

"Genes," Teague said. "G-E-N-E-S. You know, DNA? Not your trousers, you big boof."

"Right," Brody said. "Leave it to you to get all scientific on us, Dr. Einstein."

"So, Casanova, what do you propose we do about this mess?" Teague asked.

Brody shrugged. "Why do you think you should do anything? Gemma and Hayley went home. Obviously they weren't interested in living out here in the middle of nowhere. Do you blame them? Our own mother couldn't handle it. Why would they even try?"

"It's not that bad," Callum said, leaning forward in his saddle to look at Brody. "Payton likes it here."

"She does," Brody agreed. "With Teague over at Wallaroo all the time, you're going to need some help running the place. We thought we'd stick around and give you a hand."

"But you're going to take the tryout, right?" Cal's expression turned serious. "You can't give up that chance."

Brody nodded. "Once the knee is stronger."

"Hell, if I could pick this station up and move it to Ireland, I'd do it straightaway," Callum said. "Without a second thought." He turned to Teague. "And you. Why should you even be worried? Hayley has a job in Sydney. At least for a few more months. If that's not enough time to convince her to move in with you, then you're not as smooth as I thought you were."

Callum was right. At least he and Brody had more

options. Cal was pretty much stuck. He'd never walk away from the station. He'd dreamed about running Kerry Creek since he was a kid. But then, he'd never been in love before.

"Maybe you ought to try and convince Gemma to come back," Teague said. "Go to Ireland. Explain to her how you feel and ask her to come home with you."

Callum shook his head. "She wouldn't want to live here."

"Why not? If she loves you, she probably won't care where you live. And Brody and I can watch over the station while you're gone."

"No, I'm fine."

"What did she say when you asked her to stay?" Brody inquired.

Callum frowned. "I didn't ask. She had to go home. She didn't have a choice. Besides, I didn't want to deal with the rejection."

"Jaysus, Cal," Brody and Teague said in unison.

"You don't get anything unless you ask." Teague chuckled. "This is the problem. You've been trapped on this station for so long, you've never learned to deal with women. You are completely clueless."

"If you know all the right moves, then why are you alone?" Cal countered.

"Point taken," Teague muttered.

"I have an idea," Callum said. He pushed his hat down on his head. "Follow me." With a raucous whoop, Callum kicked his horse, and the gelding took off at a gallop. Teague and Brody looked at each other, then did the same, following after him in a cloud of dust and pounding hooves.

Teague assumed they were going to Kerry Creek for a few coldies and some brotherly commiserating. But instead, Callum veered north. As they came over a low rise, he saw the big rock and instantly knew what his brother had planned.

Brody looked over at him and laughed, then urged his horse ahead, overtaking Callum to reach the rock first. He threw himself out of the saddle and scrambled to the top, waiting as Teague and Callum approached.

Brody gave them both a hand up and when they were all standing on top of the rock, he nodded. "Doesn't seem as big as it used to, does it?"

Teague couldn't believe it, either. The rock had once seemed like a mountain, but now he could understand how it might have been rolled here from another spot. "So what do we do? I'm not sure I remember."

"We have to say it out loud," Callum replied. "One wish. The thing you want most in the world."

"How do we know it will work?" Teague asked.

"It worked for me. Remember? I wished I could be a pro footballer. And it happened."

"And I wished I could run a station like Kerry Creek," Callum said. "And I'm running Kerry Creek. I remember what you wished for. You wanted a plane."

"Or a helicopter," Brody said. "I guess you got your wish, too."

"So what makes you think it will work again?" Teague asked.

"We won't know unless we try." Callum drew a deep breath. "I wish Gemma would come back to Kerry Creek for good."

"I wish Hayley would realize I'm the only guy she will ever love."

"I wish Payton would say yes when I ask her to marry me," Brody said.

Teague and Callum looked over at him in astonishment and Brody grinned. "You don't get anything in life unless you ask."

"Well, I guess that's it," Callum said in his usual down-to-business manner. "We'll see if it works. Are you riding back to Kerry Creek with us?"

"I've got work to do on Wallaroo," he said. "But I'll come by tomorrow to talk about our deal."

They jumped off the rock and remounted their horses. Then Brody and Callum headed toward Kerry Creek and Teague toward Wallaroo. The ride to the homestead was filled with thoughts of Hayley. She'd left for L.A. four days ago and he hadn't heard from her since. He'd tracked down her phone number and tried calling, but had gotten her voice mail and hung up.

He thought if she answered, he would know what to say. Something would come to him. But he couldn't leave a message. So he called occasionally, hoping that she'd answer. And when she did, he'd be able to put into words how he felt about her.

But didn't she already know how he felt? Hadn't he made it clear? Or, like Cal, had he forgotten to ask her to stay? He rewound every one of their conversations. No, he'd asked, over and over. And she'd refused.

"Guess I'll have to find a better way to convince her," he murmured.

When he reached the stable, he groomed and fed Tapper then sent him out into the yard with Molly and two other horses he'd brought over from Kerry Creek. As he got the operation running, he'd bring over more and more stock until all the breeding mares were stabled at Wallaroo.

There were still repairs to make on the paddock fences and supplies to buy. Between working on the house and the stables, he spent his time making calls, flying out of Wallaroo and returning each evening before sunset. The airstrip on Wallaroo was much closer to the house than the one on Kerry Creek had been, and he'd considered running electricity out for some crude landing lights. Then he wouldn't have to worry about the length of his workday.

But that was a project for a later date. There were too many things to be done. He strode to the house, slowing his pace when he reached the porch. He'd managed to paint the facade a bright white and the trim a deep green. When he'd chosen the colors, he'd thought about what Hayley might have picked and wished she'd been there with him. But without her input, he'd depended on an old color photo of the place.

It looked good. In fact, he couldn't remember ever seeing the house looking quite that nice. He planned to get flowers and bushes for around the porch in spring. And he'd put a porch swing up and buy some comfortable chairs so they could—

"They," he repeated out loud. He was still thinking in terms of "they." He and Hayley, together on Wallaroo. It was always good to be optimistic, but when did optimism turn into delusion? "Give her three months," Teague said. "No, six." After that, he'd be forced to come to terms with the possibility that she wouldn't come back.

He pulled open the front door and walked inside. The interior smelled like fresh paint. He'd finished the front parlor and rearranged the furniture, bringing over his favorite chair from his room at Kerry Creek.

He walked across the parlor to the small desk that Harry had used to keep the accounts for the station. He'd been meaning to go though the papers and see if there was anything he should keep.

Grabbing a chair, he sat down and started with the top drawer. He pulled it out, then dumped it at his feet. A packet of letters caught his attention and he picked them up and examined the envelope on the top.

His breath caught as he recognized his name and his old address at Murdoch University, all written in Hayley's careless scrawl. He slipped the string off the packet and flipped through each envelope. There were letters to him and from him, all of them unopened.

Teague rose and walked out the front door to the porch. He sat down on the step and opened a letter in his handwriting.

As he read the text, memories flooded his mind, memories of a nervous teenager, alone in a strange city, wishing he was home with the girl he loved. Teague chuckled at the clumsy declarations of love, the silly questions, the assurances that they'd be together again soon.

Harry had obviously intercepted his letters, probably meeting the mail plane himself each week. And he'd obviously searched through the outgoing mail for Hayley's letters, as well. Teague had never imagined her grandfather might interfere with the mail. Would things have been different if the letters had been delivered? There was no way of knowing.

He opened a letter from Hayley, written on stationery he'd given her right before he left, stationery decorated with an ink drawing of a horse. It was nearly the same as his letter, declarations of affection and news of her days on Wallaroo.

He stared out across the yard. It was a bit ironic. Now he was the one left waiting and wondering when he'd see her again, hoping for any type of communication. "Come home, Hayley," he said softly. "Come home soon."

HAYLEY'S EYES drifted closed. She shook herself awake and squinted at the deserted road in front of her. She'd landed in Sydney about fifteen hours earlier. She'd lost an entire day on the trip back, but she'd managed to sleep most of the way home. After landing, she'd packed the car and headed north on the Pacific Highway.

A breakfast stop outside of Brisbane provided the opportunity for a short nap before heading west toward

Bilbarra and Wallaroo. The drive had been pleasant when she'd made it a month ago. She'd taken her time, traveling over two days, rather than driving straight through.

But she was anxious to get home, to see Teague again and to try to repair the damage she'd done by leaving. They hadn't spoken for a week and Hayley hadn't bothered to call and warn him of her arrival. She didn't want to explain her actions. She just wanted to walk up to him, throw herself into his arms and kiss him until she was certain he understood how she felt.

She felt like a fool for leaving him in the first place. Teague had put up with a lot of foolish behavior from her, but she hoped he would forgive this one last mistake. She wasn't about to walk away again, at least not until they'd come to an understanding.

They needed to discuss whether they would live together at Wallaroo as friends, as lovers or as two people who were planning to spend the rest of their lives together. Hayley preferred the latter, but she was willing to settle for the other two choices.

As she passed the road to Kerry Creek, she slowed her car, wondering if she ought to stop there first. Over the past week, she'd wondered if Teague had changed his mind about living on Wallaroo. The house was a wreck and it would be a lonely place to live compared to the hustle and bustle of his family's station.

If he wasn't at Wallaroo, she'd take the time to clean up, maybe catch a few hours of sleep and then drive over to see him later in the day. She glanced in the rearview mirror then groaned at the sight she saw.

Dark shadows smudged the skin beneath her eyes and her hair was a mess of tangles. The makeup she'd worn for her audition was long since gone. She hoped he'd be so happy to have her home he wouldn't notice the details of her appearance.

As she drove down the road to Wallaroo, her energy began to surge and she felt a jolt of adrenaline kick in. She was about to change the course of her life for the second time. Only this time, she was steering directly toward what she'd left behind.

She stopped the car at the end of the long driveway into Wallaroo, then got out and retrieved her bag from the rear seat. She tugged off her T-shirt and jeans and slipped on a soft cotton dress. Then she found her brush and tamed her unruly hair, tying it back with a scarf.

When she bent down to look at her reflection in the side mirror, she thought about lipstick and a bit of mascara, but then decided against it. Teague had always preferred her without makeup. She didn't want to look like Hayley, the television star. She wanted to look like Hayley, the girl he'd fallen in love with years before.

Gathering her resolve, she hopped back into the car and started off down the driveway. As she got closer to the house, she noticed something odd. It seemed to gleam in the morning sun. It was only when she entered the yard that Hayley realized the house had been painted.

A tiny gasp slipped from her lips. The two-story clapboard structure looked so shiny and new she barely recognized it. Teague had painted the trim around the windows and the porch floor a deep green. And she noticed a row of new green shutters drying in the sun.

She stopped the car and slowly got out, taking in the other changes that had been made in the course of a week. The yard was clean and raked, the various bits of junk that had collected over the years hauled away. Teague had dug up the ground along the front side of the porch as if to make a garden. And the weather vane that had once perched on the roof at a precarious angle was now fixed and functional.

The front door was open and she peered through the screen, wondering if Teague was inside. She hesitantly opened the screen door, calling out his name, but the house was silent. Hayley looked around in astonishment. He'd worked miracles on the interior, as well. The walls had been painted and the woodwork had been oiled. The plank floors now gleamed with a fresh coat of wax and all the furniture had been rearranged.

It was Wallaroo as it had been, back in its early days, when everything was bright and new, back in the days when her grandmother had been alive and this had been a real home. She walked into the parlor and sat down in a soft leather chair, a chair she recognized from Teague's bedroom at Kerry Creek.

Hayley noticed a pile of mail on the table nearby and reached for it. A tiny sigh slipped from her lips as she realized what she was holding. Her letters to Teague! They were all here, all neatly addressed with the stamps unmarked. She pulled one out of the envelope and read it, each word ringing in her mind as if it had been yesterday.

"I found them in Harry's desk drawer."

She glanced up to see Teague watching her from behind the screen door. He was dressed in work clothes, his stockman's hat pulled low over his eyes. She couldn't read his expression and didn't know if he was pleased or displeased that she'd returned.

Hayley slowly stood and dropped the letters onto the chair. "Hi," she said.

"Hi, yourself," he replied.

"I'm back." She swallowed hard. It wasn't sparkling conversation, but it was the best she could manage between her pounding heart and her dizzy head.

"I can see that."

"I thought I should come home."

"To check up on me?"

She frowned. "No. I mean, yes. To see you. I wanted to see you."

"Why are you here, Hayley?"

She sighed impatiently. "Can we at least be standing in the same room when we have this conversation?"

"What conversation is that?"

"The one where I tell you that I was stupid to leave and that I'm in love with you and I hope you're in love with me." The words came out in a rush and after she said them all, she felt a warm blush creep up her cheeks. So what if it hadn't been scriptworthy romantic dialogue. This wasn't a scene from a television program, this was real life. And real life wasn't perfect.

"Say that again," he murmured.

"No," she said. "Not until you come inside."

He reached for the door, then thought better of it. "I'm going to stay out here."

"Why?"

"Because if I come inside, I'm going to have to kiss you. And once I start, I'm not sure I'm going to be able to stop."

"That sounds nice," Hayley said, smiling at him. "Please come inside." She walked to the door and pushed open the screen door. "Come on." She stepped aside to let him pass. But as he did, his arm slipped around her waist and he pulled her against him.

In a heartbeat, his mouth came down on hers in a deep and soul-searching kiss. He left no doubt about his feelings. In a single instant, Hayley knew he was glad she'd returned. She ran her hands over his shoulders and arms, enjoying the feel of his body. She hadn't realized how much she'd missed touching him.

Teague scooped her up in his arms and walked into the parlor. She grabbed his hat and tossed it aside, taking in the details of his handsome face as they continued kissing. He sat down in the leather chair, settling her on his lap, molding her mouth to his until she felt as if she might pass out.

Hayley smiled as she teased him with tiny kisses, first on his mouth, then his jaw and finally on his neck. "So you're happy to have me home."

"That depends on how long you're planning to stay."

"I was thinking maybe the rest of my life." She looked up at him.

He drew back, then held her face between his hands. "What does that mean?"

"Exactly what I said. This is my home now. I'm going to come and go from Wallaroo. I'll have to return to Sydney to finish up my contract on *Castle Cove*. Then I'll sell my place and move everything up here."

A grin broke over his face. "You're going to live here with me," he said, as if to reassure himself that he'd heard her right.

"Yes. It's my house, too."

"What about your career?"

"Well, if something interesting comes along, then we'll discuss it. We may need money for buying stock. Or for fixing up the station. I'm not going to make any plans right now, except to spend the next week with you. Then I have to go back."

"We have a week? What will we do with ourselves?" He cupped her breast.

"You'll have to work and I'm sure I'll find something to do around here." She chuckled.

"About that. Work, I mean. I spoke with Doc Daley and we've made a few changes in our plans. I'm not going to take over his practice, at least not all of it. I'm going to do the equine cases only, so I can spend more time on the station. And he's going to find someone else to take over the rest of the work. I figured, if we wanted to make a go of Wallaroo, I needed to be here as much as possible."

"So, I guess it's all settled then. You and I are business partners."

"And friends," he said.

"Lovers, too," Hayley added.

"Roommates."

She smiled. "Soul mates."

"And the rest will come," he assured her. He ran his fingers through her hair and pulled her into another kiss, lingering over her mouth. "I love you, Hayley. I always have and I always will."

"And I love you, Teague."

He smoothed his fingers through her hair. "You must be very tired from your trip. I can tell you'd like to lie down."

"Oh, you can tell?" she teased. "I think you want to get me into the bedroom."

"Actually, I want to show you the bed." He stood and pulled her along to the upstairs, past the door to Harry's old room, past the door to her room, to the largest of the bedrooms. Harry had used it for storage, like an attic, filling it full of old furniture and things he couldn't bear to throw away. She'd always suspected it was the room he'd shared with her grandmother. The beautiful bedroom set was too fancy for a single man to use.

But Teague had cleaned the room out. The old bed was there, but dressed with brand-new linens. He tossed her onto it, then flopped down beside her. "Do you like it?"

"Yes." She turned and ran her hands over the down

comforter. It was exactly like the— "These are the bed linens from the resort."

"I liked them so much that I bought some. They sell the bed linens and the soap and the shampoo right from the hotel. I bought the sheets and the down comforter. Oh, and the down pillows. And I got one of those nice showerheads, too."

Hayley rolled over and threw her arms out. "It's perfect. I could spend all day in this bed."

"Is that a request or a demand? Because I'd be quite happy to keep you in this bed all day."

She rolled over and wrapped her arms around his neck, remembering that first day at the big rock. He'd saved her life that day. Without Teague, Hayley probably wouldn't have survived her teenage years. But he'd made every day an adventure, every moment something wonderful to be shared.

"Promise me you'll love me forever," she said.

"I will love you forever and beyond," Teague said, his declaration simple and direct and honest.

"My life starts today," Hayley said. "No more fears, no more running away. And if I ever get a little crazy again, I want you to drag me back into this bedroom and prove to me why we belong together."

"Can I do that now?" Teague asked.

Hayley laughed, then kissed his mouth. "Yes," she said. "And don't stop doing it until I tell you."

As Teague began to seduce her, Hayley closed her eyes and gave herself over to the man she loved. How something so complicated had suddenly turned so simple, she would never understand. It was like a switch had been thrown and a light turned on, illuminating all the things she knew deep in her heart yet had never acknowledged.

She was exactly where she belonged now—in Teague's arms. And after so many years of searching, she was finally home.

* * * * *

There's only one single Quinn brother left.
Callum's head over heels for Gemma,
but what will he do when he learns she has
a secret that could change his life forever?
Find out in the final
QUINNS DOWN UNDER *book,*
available next month.

*Celebrate 60 years of pure
reading pleasure with Harlequin!*

To commemorate the event, Harlequin Intrigue®
is thrilled to invite you to the wedding of The Colby
Agency's J. T. Baxley and his bride, Eve Mattson.

That is, of course, if J.T. can find the woman who
left him at the altar. Considering he's a private
investigator for one of the top agencies in the
country—the best of the best—that shouldn't be
a problem. The real setback is that his bride isn't
who she appears to be…and her mysterious past
has put them both in danger.

*Enjoy an exclusive glimpse of
Debra Webb's latest addition to*
THE COLBY AGENCY:
ELITE RECONNAISSANCE DIVISION

THE BRIDE'S SECRETS

*Available August 2009
from Harlequin Intrigue®.*

The dark figures on the dock were still firing. The bullets cutting through the surface of the water without the warning boom of shots told Eve they were using silencers.

That was to her benefit. Silencers decreased the accuracy of every shot and lessened the range.

She grabbed for the rocks. Scrambled through the darkness. Bumped her knee on a boulder. Cursed.

Burrowing into the waist-deep grass, she kept low and crawled forward. Faster. Pushed harder. Needed as much distance as possible.

Shots pinged on the rocks.

J.T. scrambled alongside her.

He was breathing hard.

They had to stay close to the ground until they reached the next row of warehouses. Even though she was relatively certain they were out of range at this point, she wasn't taking any risks. And she wasn't slowing down.

J.T. had to keep up.

The splat of a bullet hitting the ground next to Eve had her rolling left. Maybe they weren't completely out of range.

She bumped J.T. He grunted.

His injured arm. Dammit. She could apologize later.

Half a dozen more yards.

Almost in the clear.

As she reached the cover of the alley between the first two warehouses she tensed.

Silence.

No pings or splats.

She glanced back at the dock. Deserted.

Time to run.

Her car was parked another block down.

Pushing to her feet, she sprinted forward. The wet bag dragged at her shoulder. She ignored it.

By the time she reached the lot where her car was parked, she had dug the keys from her pocket and hit the fob. Six seconds later she was behind the wheel. She hit the ignition as J.T. collapsed into the passenger seat. Tires squealed as she spun out of the slot.

"What the hell did you do to me?"

From the corner of her eye she watched him shake his head in an attempt to clear it.

He would be pissed when she told him about the tranquilizer.

She'd needed him cooperative until she formulated a plan. A drug-induced state of unconsciousness had been the fastest and most efficient method to ensure his continued solidarity.

"I can't really talk right now." Eve weaved into the right lane as the street widened to four lanes. What she needed was traffic. It was Saturday night—shouldn't be that difficult to find as soon as they were out of the old warehouse district.

A glance in the rearview mirror warned that their unwanted company had caught up.

Sensing her tension, J.T. turned to peer over his left shoulder.

"I hope you have a plan B."

She shot him a look. "There's always plan G." Then she pulled the Glock out of her waistband.

Cutting the steering wheel left, she slid between two vehicles. Another veer to the right and she'd put several cars between hers and the enemy.

She was betting they wouldn't pull out the firepower in the open like this, but a girl could never be too sure when it came to an unknown enemy.

Deep blending was the way to go.

Two traffic lights ahead the marquis of a movie theater provided exactly the opportunity she was looking for.

The digital numbers on the dash indicated it was just past midnight. Perfect timing. The late movie would be purging its audience into the crowd of teenagers who liked hanging out in the parking lot.

She took a hard right onto the property that sported a twelve-screen theater, numerous fast-food hot spots and a chain superstore. Speeding across the lot, she selected a lane of parking slots. Pulling in as close to the theater entrance as possible, she shut off the engine and reached for her door.

"Let's go."

Thankfully he didn't argue.

Rounding the hood of her car, she shoved the Glock into her bag, then wrapped her arm around J.T.'s and merged into the crowd.

With her free hand she finger-combed her long hair. It was soaked, as were her clothes. The kids she bumped into noticed, gave her death-ray glares.

They just didn't know.

As she and J.T. moved in closer to the building, she grabbed a baseball cap from an innocent bystander. The crowd made it easy. The kid who owned the cap had made it even easier by stuffing the cap bill-first into his waistband at the small of his back.

Pushing through the loitering crowd, she made her way to the side of the building next to the main entrance. She pushed J.T. against the wall and dropped her bag to the ground. Peeled off her tee and let it fall.

His gaze instantly zeroed in on her breasts, where the cami she wore had glued to her skin like an extra layer. A zing of desire shot through her veins.

Not the time.

With a flick of her wrist she twisted her hair up and clamped the cap atop the blond mass.

"They're coming," J.T. muttered as he gazed at some point beyond her.

"Yeah, I know." She planted her palms against the

wall on either side of him and leaned in. "Keep your eyes open. Let me know when they're inside."

Then she planted her lips on his.

* * * * *

Will J.T. and Eve be caught in the moment?
Or will Eve get the chance to
reveal all of her secrets?
Find out in
THE BRIDE'S SECRETS
by Debra Webb.
Available August 2009
from Harlequin Intrigue®.

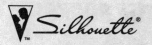

REQUEST YOUR FREE BOOKS!

2 FREE NOVELS PLUS 2 FREE GIFTS!

HARLEQUIN®

Blaze™

Red-hot reads!

YES! Please send me 2 FREE Harlequin® Blaze™ novels and my 2 FREE gifts (gifts are worth about $10). After receiving them, if I don't wish to receive any more books, I can return the shipping statement marked "cancel". If I don't cancel, I will receive 6 brand-new novels every month and be billed just $4.24 per book in the U.S. or $4.71 per book in Canada. That's a savings of 15% off the cover price. It's quite a bargain. Shipping and handling is just 50¢ per book.* I understand that accepting the 2 free books and gifts places me under no obligation to buy anything. I can always return a shipment and cancel at any time. Even if I never buy another book, the two free books and gifts are mine to keep forever.

151 HDN EYS2   351 HDN EYTE

Name	(PLEASE PRINT)	
Address		Apt. #
City	State/Prov.	Zip/Postal Code

Signature (if under 18, a parent or guardian must sign)

Mail to the **Harlequin Reader Service:**
IN U.S.A.: P.O. Box 1867, Buffalo, NY 14240-1867
IN CANADA: P.O. Box 609, Fort Erie, Ontario L2A 5X3

Not valid to current subscribers of Harlequin Blaze books.

Want to try two free books from another line?
Call 1-800-873-8635 or visit www.morefreebooks.com.

* Terms and prices subject to change without notice. Prices do not include applicable taxes. N.Y. residents add applicable sales tax. Canadian residents will be charged applicable provincial taxes and GST. Offer not valid in Quebec. This offer is limited to one order per household. All orders subject to approval. Credit or debit balances in a customer's account(s) may be offset by any other outstanding balance owed by or to the customer. Please allow 4 to 6 weeks for delivery. Offer available while quantities last.

Your Privacy: Harlequin Books is committed to protecting your privacy. Our Privacy Policy is available online at www.eHarlequin.com or upon request from the Reader Service. From time to time we make our lists of customers available to reputable third parties who may have a product or service of interest to you. If you would prefer we not share your name and address, please check here. ☐

HB09R3

You're invited to join our Tell Harlequin Reader Panel!

By joining our new reader panel you will:

- Receive Harlequin® books—they are FREE and yours to keep with no obligation to purchase anything!
- Participate in fun online surveys
- Exchange opinions and ideas with women just like you
- Have a say in our new book ideas and help us publish the best in women's fiction

In addition, you will have a chance to win great prizes and receive special gifts!
See Web site for details. Some conditions apply. Space is limited.

To join, visit us at
www.TellHarlequin.com.

HARLEQUIN Blaze™

COMING NEXT MONTH
Available July 28, 2009

#483 UNBRIDLED Tori Carrington
After being arrested for a crime he didn't commit, former Marine Carter Southard is staying far away from the one thing that's always gotten him into trouble—women! Unfortunately, his sexy new attorney, Laney Cartwright, is making that very difficult....

#484 THE PERSONAL TOUCH Lori Borrill
Professional matchmaker Margot Roth needs to give her latest client the personal touch—property mogul Clint Hilton is a playboy extraordinaire and is looking for a date...for his mother. But while Margot's setting up mom, Clint decides Margot's for him. Let the seduction begin!

#485 HOT UNDER PRESSURE Kathleen O'Reilly
Where You Least Expect It
Ashley Larsen and David McLean are hot for each other. Who knew the airport would be the perfect place to find the perfect sexual partner? But can the lust last when it's a transcontinental journey every time these two want to hook up?

#486 SLIDING INTO HOME Joanne Rock
Encounters
Take me out to the ball game... Four sexy major leaguers are duking it out for the ultimate prize—the Golden Glove award. Little do they guess that the women fate puts in their path will offer them even more of a challenge...and a much more satisfying reward!

#487 STORM WATCH Jill Shalvis
Uniformly Hot!
During his stint in the National Guard, Jason Mauer had seen his share of natural disasters. But when he finds himself in a flash flood with an old crush—sexy Lizzy Mann—the waves of desire turn out to be too much....

#488 THE MIGHTY QUINNS: CALLUM Kate Hoffmann
Quinns Down Under
Gemma Moynihan's sexy Irish eyes are smiling on Callum Quinn! Charming the ladies has never been quiet Cal's style. But he plans to charm the pants off luscious Gemma—until he finds out she's keeping a dangerous secret...

www.eHarlequin.com

HBCNMBPA0709